THE US Review of Books

The Ambassador's Daughter
reviewed by John E. Roper

"The militiamen immediately seized the girls. All of them gasped for air, shocked that they were singled out and in fear of what lay ahead."

It was supposed to be an exotic vacation, a chance for Renée Davis and her friends from college to take a break during the summer and see the sights in South Africa where Renée's father has been appointed as the United States' Ambassador. But much of that racially-divided nation is still in turmoil, as the country has only recently transitioned from the apartheid system and has elected its first black president, Nelson Mandela. In an attempt to gain some leverage with the new government and force it to meet its demands, a militant cabal decides to play a dangerous game, one that will use Renée and her companions as helpless pawns.

The author blends historical fact with a heavy dose of fiction to craft his political drama. For example, while Mandela and F.W. de Klerk are well known figures from South African history, Williams chooses to create fictional politicians for the United States during the same period, possibly due to their roles being more active in the story. Likewise, real-life organizations such as the Inkatha Freedom Party and the Afrikaner Volksfront play major parts in the narrative, but Zulu leaders such as Musa Goba and Welton Betelema, along with the white separatist leader Verdi Piethro Higgs, are simply products of the author's imagination. However, when the book is read more as an action novel rather than traditional historical fiction, these issues become minor. And as an action novel William's tale has a lot going for it. A sympathetic heroine, a vile antagonist in Higgs, and a plethora of military action combine to make the author's debut book a good choice for an evening's entertainment.

Pacific Book Review

Reviewed by: Joe Kilgore

Novels that blend fact and fiction often have added allure because they are able to leverage events that have already peaked reader's interest. However, by necessity, they must also blend fictional constructs with factual events in a way that is not only entertaining, but also credible. Author Harvey J. Williams attempts to pull off such sleight of hand in his debut novel, *The Ambassador's Daughter.*

He begins by providing a prologue that details the horrific violence leading up to the first free all-race elections held in South Africa. The end of Apartheid in 1993, while celebrated by most people inside and outside that country, was also opposed by a number of warring factions that feared the loss of status, property, and power. That fear of loss is the axis on which Mr. William's thriller turns.

As negotiations are being finalized for celebrations that will usher in the country's election and their first constitution, Horace Davis, the first U. S. Ambassador to South Africa, along with other high-ranking dignitaries, are planning to take part in the event. Davis' daughter, a college student at UCLA, will be flying there with three of her friends to join her father and mother for the festivities. But other plans are afoot as well; rival political organizations are exploring schemes to disrupt the transition to a new South African government. One plan even calls for the kidnapping of the American Ambassador's daughter. Though the idea is initially rejected, rogue military elements within the organizations join forces to carry out the plan anyway.

What follows is high adventure as the plotters pull off a daring airline hijacking. They abduct the daughter and her friends away to a hidden terrorist training center and plan to use them as bargaining chips in their attempt to subvert the country's move to democracy. Unknown to the conspirators however, eyes-in-the-sky have zeroed in on their location, and soon an International Special Forces team is being assembled to attempt a daring rescue.

Suspense mounts as time is running down to meet the kidnapper's demands. Treachery intercedes as someone on the Ambassador's household staff alerts the militants to what is underway. The bad guys adjust - the good guys revise. Before you know it, a fierce battle is underway and everyone's life hangs in the balance.

Mr. Williams has a firm grasp of both the history and the various participants involved in the death of Apartheid and the violent birth of the new South Africa. He is on somewhat shakier ground as he struggles to keep his prose pithy and his story tight and hardhitting. He has chosen a historical environment for his first novel that provides inherent interest; readers will have to decide for themselves if the fiction lives up to the facts.

THE AMBASSADOR'S
DAUGHTER

HARVEY J. WILLIAMS

iUniverse®

THE AMBASSADOR'S DAUGHTER

iUniverse books may be ordered through booksellers or by contacting:

iUniverse
1663 Liberty Drive
Bloomington, IN 47403
www.iuniverse.com
1-800-Authors (1-800-288-4677)

Because of the dynamic nature of the Internet, any web addresses or links contained in this book may have changed since publication and may no longer be valid. The views expressed in this work are solely those of the author and do not necessarily reflect the views of the publisher, and the publisher hereby disclaims any responsibility for them.

Any people depicted in stock imagery provided by Thinkstock are models, and such images are being used for illustrative purposes only. Certain stock imagery © Thinkstock.

ISBN: 978-1-4917-4219-8 (sc)
ISBN: 978-1-4917-4220-4 (hc)
ISBN: 978-1-4917-4221-1 (e)

Library of Congress Control Number: 2014913112

Print information available on the last page.

iUniverse rev. date: 11/21/2016

In loving memory of my dad, Reverend Harry W. Williams, and to my very vibrant, wise, 101-year-old mom, Mrs. Iva A. Williams, both of whom stressed education as a vehicle for success and did not allow me to say "I can't" but rather "I will do my best."

To the memory of Nelson Mandela and the many brave men and women who struggled with him for so long for the abolition of apartheid and the march to freedom in South Africa.

ACKNOWLEDGMENTS

Writing your first book is truly an eye-opener for the novice writer. An endeavor that I thought would take a few months has stretched out to a few years. There was so much to learn, and many people helped along the way. I especially want to thank my daughter Nichole for editing the book, helping with the cover design, and giving her unique enthusiasm and encouragement throughout the process. My entire family was encouraging.

Thank you to my wife, Beverly Williams, Esq., who read and critiqued the original transcript and prepared all the legal aspects of the book's first publication.

To my daughters Nitalya and Natasha. Nitalya not only contributed as the photographer for the book cover, photographing Natasha who participated as a model, but also posed for the photo of one of the main characters, Renée.

To my son, Steve, and his wife, Kym, for showing excitement and interest.

Thank you also to Stephanie Dubois for her support, information, and final editing of the first edition of my novel.

Thank you to Marlene, Glenda, Jean, Ethyl, and all others who helped in the development of *The Ambassador's Daughter*.

Thanks to the iUniverse staff for guiding me through the editing and publishing of this edition of *The Ambassador's Daughter*.

INTRODUCTION

As I watched and followed the developments in the historic struggle of the South African people in trying to throw off the shackles of apartheid, and the release of the ANC leader Nelson Mandela and his subsequent election as the first president of South Africa in which all races participated, I wanted to somehow participate in this historic event. I was both proud of and scared for South Africa because I was aware of the many obstacles that this new democracy had to overcome, including South Africa's history.

In 1910, the Union of South Africa was formed. Though weak economically and dependent on foreign capital, 1,250,000 enfranchised whites took political control over 4,250,000 Africans, 500,000 coloreds, and 165,000 East Indians. Apartheid—racial separation, with white political domain—was the political system. This system of oppression was brutally enforced by the military, the police, the justice system, and all enfranchised political parties.

In the 1950s, black African reformists and revolutionaries began to actively resist apartheid in South Africa, along with liberal white organizations. The African National Congress (ANC) and the Pan-African Congress, after being banned by the South African Parliament, went underground to continue the struggle to end to apartheid in South Africa.

After decades of armed conflict and the deaths of thousands of its citizens, the all-white South African Parliament voted to end apartheid by adopting a new constitution that included equal voting rights for all of its people, white, black, colored, Indian, and others. Apartheid officially ended on December 22, 1993.

Many factions did not accept this new transition from apartheid to democracy, and they vowed to secede from South Africa to form their own independent states. Several Afrikaner-led factions joined together to continue to resist these changes. The Inkatha Zulu Party called for an independent Zulu state in Natal Homelands. Apartheid was not going to dissolve quietly or easily; the struggle continued.

I read about the struggle that was taking place and decided to write this novel. This novel is based on some of the events that occurred before the free all-race elections as reported in newspapers, periodicals, and magazines throughout the world.

Prologue

On a Sunday night in Warmbad, a right-wing proapartheid stronghold north of Pretoria, a powerful bomb blew up a daycare center for black South African children. Surrounding buildings and homes were damaged. Offices and homes of the black-led African National Congress had been previous targets of the bombers.

At four in the morning, the commuter train carrying thousands of black South Africans to their jobs in Johannesburg was moving slowly down the tracks. People were reading newspapers, exchanging greetings, and having conversations. The main topics of the conversations were the fast-moving events in South African politics and the violence that was accompanying the changes. The people were polite and congenial to each other on the ride. There was a hint of the sun rising, and the morning was very peaceful. Suddenly, a tremendous explosion rocked the train, damaging and derailing the front cars. The train ran off the tracks, injuring hundreds of commuters and killing many in the ensuing turmoil.

A rich, conservative white Afrikaner opposed to the all-race elections took credit for this terrorist attack.

Iniwe, South Africa

Zanaiah Milithuli's Umemulo, a traditional Zulu ritual to mark a young man's coming of age had almost ended. He and his friends had danced in celebration and bathed in a river, a cow had been slaughtered for the feast, and everyone had drunk bottle after bottle of beer.

While he was sitting with his family around a fire, recounting the events of the day, without warning, killers came with AK-47 assault rifles and blasted away at them. When the shooting stopped, Milithuli and seven other family members, including a four-year-old boy and a six-year-old girl, were dead. A survivor of the massacre could only remember that the terrorists took their time firing round after round and clip after clip into the family gathering. Scores of spent cartridges were found on the ground. They fired additional shots in the air in triumph as they ran across a shallow river and cornfields to a rival village on a nearby hill.

Zulu attacked Zulu, and Inkatha followers attacked ANC followers. ANC followers attacked Inkatha Freedom followers. Both groups were bitter rivals. The Inkatha Freedom Party vowed to disrupt free all-race elections in South Africa and to not recognize them because their archenemy's leader was heavily favored to be elected as the first black African president of South Africa. In addition, most parliamentary seats and provincial government houses were slated to be captured by the hated ANC.

This rivalry resulted in a low-intensity civil war between the ANC and the Inkatha Freedom Party with the IFP's leader and its king calling for a Kwazulu state in Zululand located in Natal Province. This state was to have self-rule separate from the South African government.

Because of the intense hostility between the ANC and the Inkatha Freedom Party, the stakes were very high. Their opposition, aggravated by traditional clan feuds and land disputes, was the most significant cause of the violence that had left more than seventeen thousand people dead in the ten years before the end of apartheid.

The chief of the Inkatha Freedom Party had aligned his organization of Zulu Nationalists with the white supremacists, Afrikaners, Volkstaat (homeland) advocates, and conservative dictatorial black homeland leaders who had come together to fight the all-race elections. These leaders were afraid they would lose all their power and privilege under the democratic government that would replace apartheid.

Worshippers had crowded into the pews of the multiracial St. James Church in Cape Town. Many were praying for the end of all the violence that had encompassed all of South Africa during the turbulent transition from apartheid to democracy. The minister was speaking to the congregation about this subject when nail-studded grenades came crashing through the windows, exploding and killing or wounding scores of worshippers. Black South African men broke through the doors and sprayed the congregation with automatic weapons for several minutes before fleeing the scene. More than fifty people were wounded or killed.

Raymond Bleuthili, his son, and several of their friends were returning from an ANC rally in Johannesburg. They were driving home to Soweto, the largest black township near Johannesburg. They were in two cars, talking and laughing about the events of the day. It was late, about ten thirty, and they were anxious to get home.

Raymond looked in his rearview mirror and noticed that four cars had appeared behind them on the lonely stretch of rural road. They were coming up pretty fast, and he moved his car over a bit so they could pass. However, instead of passing, they came right up to his rear bumper and cruised behind him.

Raymond said, "Hey, these guys must be drunk or something." He glanced at his sleeping eleven-year old son, patted him on the head, and continued to drive his old sedan down the road.

The first vehicle behind him pulled ahead, passed his friend's car, and then slowed down. Two of the other cars moved up close to his rear bumper and positioned themselves to the side of their two cars. The fourth car stayed behind, pinning them.

Raymond knew this meant trouble. The car in the rear slammed into Raymond's bumper. The car on the side began to inch closer, forcing Raymond to move his car to the shoulder of the road. The car in front of his friend's vehicle slowed even more.

Raymond and his friends could see the white faces staring at them as the white Afrikaners ran them off the road. The cars stopped, nine white men got out, and they opened fire on the trapped black South African men and boys. When they stopped firing with nine-millimeter handguns and assault rifles, two men and Raymond's son were dead. The survivors described the attackers to police, explaining that they spoke Afrikaans and wore camouflage fatigues. One man had worn the black boots and uniform of the Iron Guard, a neo-Nazi unit that acted as bodyguards for the leader of the white supremacist Afrikaner Resistance Movement.

Bophuthatswana, one of the ten black homelands created by the apartheid government of South Africa to separate black South Africans from white South Africans, had been the scene of a bloody insurrection as the South African elections neared. Bophuthatswana's ruler and dictator, Lucas Mangope, resisted the change and wanted to keep the status quo.

The citizens of Bop, short for Bophuthatswana, wanted to vote, but Mangope would not allow it. He had ordered his army and police to resist any movement toward independence or attempts to participate in the upcoming elections for democratization of South Africa. His army and police detained, beat, and shot citizens who protested.

On a Monday, teachers joined strikers who were protesting for wage increases and pensions. The protest quickly escalated into a general anti-Mangope uprising that stopped all activity in the capital. By Thursday, many of the police and soldiers who had been firing tear gas and holding back protestors had defected and joined the protestors to rid themselves of Mangope and seize the opportunity to vote in the upcoming elections.

Mangope put out an urgent call for help to save his dictatorial rule over Bop. He called on the Afrikaner Volksfront, an alliance of white supremacist organizations, and made a pact as part of a "freedom alliance" along with the Inkatha Freedom Party. They had joined together to resist the upcoming all-race elections. Each group wanted to save its power base and retain independence.

The Volksfront stormed into Bop with between 2,000 and 5,000 white militants to save Mangope's regime. Roving bands of white supremacists were roaring down the streets of Mmabatho and firing indiscriminately at black citizens on the streets. At least two men and a woman were killed in Central Mafeking, the twin city to the capital. Cars crisscrossed the towns, chasing carloads of blacks and shooting at them. Reporters were beaten, and their film and camera equipment was taken at gunpoint.

For the entire day, gunfire could be heard throughout the city. The air was hot and still as plumes of thick black smoke billowed into the air from the barricades of burning tires and the hulks of charred cars and trucks.

Looting was widespread, and rioting and gunfire totally encompassed the capital city and the rest of the countryside. Gangs of black youths looted, cruised in cars, and randomly shot back at the white Afrikaner invaders. When the Bop police and army finally responded to the invasion, dozens of battles ensued in areas around Mmabatho and the surrounding areas.

The president of South Africa sent 1,500 South African troops to support the Bop police and army against Mangope and the Volksfront, and he pledged more if necessary. Soon after their arrival, armored personnel carriers with South African combat troops escorted convoys of white Afrikaners to the border and back to their homes. Thousands more armed Afrikaners retreated from Bophuthatswana from their stronghold next to an air force base.

The only major skirmish to follow occurred at a dusty intersection just outside of the city. Eighteen vehicles filled with white supremacists ran a roadblock that had been established by the Bop army. They fired into a crowd of black citizens near the roadblock, killing a woman.

The soldiers ordered the convoy of vehicles to stop, and a tense confrontation ensued. The air was filled with apprehension when suddenly a fierce gun battle erupted. The Bop soldiers fired continuously with assault rifles from their armored carriers. The white Afrikaners returned fire from their cars with hunting rifles, shotguns, and assault rifles. Frightened and terrified citizens and reporters scrambled for cover behind brick walls as bullets flew past.

After what seemed like an eternity, the white Afrikaners fled toward the border with the Bop soldiers in hot pursuit. All of the white supremacists' vehicles escaped—except for a blue Mercedes with three members of the Afrikaner Resistance Movement. At least eight bullets demolished the windshield and flattened a tire. One man, identified only as Dourie, died in a pool of blood on the left side of the vehicle. He wore camouflage khakis with swastika-like emblems on the sleeves.

Dave Lurys and his two companions who were captured by the Bop soldiers were from Naboomspruit, a farming town. Lurys had been shot in the arm, but he raised his arms in a sign of surrender to the Bop security forces.

Next to Lurys, Ollie Wynfort was face down. He had also been shot during the fierce exchange of gunfire. When a reporter asked why he had gone to Bop, he replied, "We came because the Afrikaner Volksfront asked us to come." Even though he'd been wounded, he did not have any regrets.

A young black South African Bop policeman in a green uniform walked up to Lurys. Without saying a word, the man shot Lurys in the chest with an assault rifle from just two feet away. The young black policeman turned and shot Ollie Wynfort in the head. Ollie and Lurys both died.

After days of looting, rioting, and deadly street fights, Lucas Mangope fled the country by helicopter. His whereabouts were unknown.

The rivalries between the ANC and Inkatha Freedom Party, fueled by ethnic differences between the Zulu and Xhosas, the two largest tribes, were blamed for four thousand deaths in 1993. A judicial report pointed to the white South African police officials as the source of arms utilized by the Inkatha Freedom Party Zulus. Their aim was to destabilize the country to prolong minority rule by the whites.

CHAPTER 1

Renée Davis was running late, and her apartment was a five-minutes drive to campus. As she got out of bed, she thought, *It was fun living in the dormitory the first two years, but I just outgrew that scene.*

Renée had convinced her mom and dad to allow her to move into an apartment with roommates for her third year. It had taken some getting used to. Renée's dorm had been noisy and full of activity, but it was nice to have peace and quiet. *Some of the time,* she thought.

Renée's two roommates could be pretty noisy, but they respected each other's privacy and study time. Mrs. Davis had flown out to be with her during the summer before junior year, and they looked for an apartment together. They found the perfect little two-bedroom, two-bathroom apartment just off Westwood and Santa Monica Boulevards. They had a lot of fun buying furniture for the apartment and found a good used car, a 1992 BMW 325i, to get around.

Shawna Johnson and Michelle Thomas, friends from the dorm, agreed to be her roommates. The roommates didn't mind sharing the big bedroom, and Renée had the smaller bedroom. It was great to be out of the dorms, and Renée loved having her own bathroom.

The spring weather was fantastic. Even though the Pacific Ocean was only five miles away, it was not too hot or humid. The weather was pretty consistent except when it would rain and be a little cooler from November through February.

Renée talked to her friends in Washington, DC, and said, "There are a plethora of places in the world that have great climates, but in the US, Southern California has the best. People who don't live in Los Angeles gripe about the problems Californians have had dealing with the big earthquakes, pollution, riots, and devastating fires, floods, mudslides—all the tragedies that have been experienced just since the nineties—but you don't see anybody moving too quickly out of LA. All anyone else has to do is watch the Rose Parade on New Year's Day, and the nice weather will influence them to move on out to sunny Southern California. With such a great climate, there is always something to do. You can go skiing in the morning, the beach in the afternoon, and the theater that night. Not to mention all the glamour and glitz of Hollywood, movie stars, and music stars."

When Renée was in high school, her parents had some business to take care of in Los Angeles, and they took Renée with them to give her an opportunity to view the campus before she made her college decision. Since Renée would be three thousand miles away from Washington, they wanted to make sure she was at least familiar with the campus before she made such a long journey away to live on her own. She had already told her parents she wanted to go to college in California. She fell in love with UCLA and was set on going to school there.

Next to UCLA, Westwood, Bel Air, and Beverly Hills were home to beautiful mansions and famous people. The school's sprawling campus was filled with rolling green hills and modern buildings. World-class professors taught in almost every classroom. There were several colleges, a technologically advanced medical center, research centers, and athletic teams.

Renée's father was the newly appointed US ambassador to South Africa. Horace L. Davis would be the first African American US ambassador to South Africa. He and Beverly Scott also had a son named Darrell.

While Renée's father was in meetings, Renée and her mom toured the campus. She had the grades in high school to go to any college. She studied hard and was involved in a lot of extracurricular activities, which were what the universities were looking for in a prospective student. They wanted well-rounded individuals who could also bring some diversity to their campuses. Not to mention that her father had a lot of political clout.

By her third year, Renée had gotten used to the school. It wasn't all that she'd thought it would be—the classes were too big, some of the professors only taught the classes once in a while, and grad students taught some classes—but she still liked it.

Renée was doing pretty well in her premed classes, and she liked the diversity of the school. Students came from all over the US and many other countries, and she had made lots of friends.

Renée got out of bed and kicked over some of the books and papers she had been studying. She hit the snooze button again and stumbled into the bathroom, groggy from not getting enough sleep over the past few days. It was finals time, and her room was an absolute mess. Books and papers were sprawled everywhere. She hadn't put them away after she'd completed each final; instead, she had just pulled out more papers and books for the next final she had to take.

Surely, Renée thought, *the papers in this room are having babies because every day they are piling up higher and higher.*

She looked in the mirror at the side of her face, which was a little sore, and was shocked to see the faint imprint of words from the book she had accidently slept on.

Staring at the imprint, she said, "Micro-bi-ol... great! I can read the answers printed on my face in my final—if I bring my compact and can read backward fast enough," she said.

Renée looked out the bathroom door toward her messy room. "Ugh," she said. She hadn't really cleaned her room since finals began and surely didn't have time to clean up now. She had to meet her study group in half an hour. She was still half asleep, but she had to take a quick shower, brush her teeth, and forget about the makeup.

Her hair was in long plaits. She had been wearing braids since the Christmas break. She was tired of dealing with her hair every morning, and she'd gotten extensions, which she loved. Up in the morning, brush the edges, and off to school! No fussing with her hair.

Renée was relatively tall; she liked to say she was five-nine. Her velvety-brown complexion, shoulder-length black hair, long black eyelashes, and honey-brown eyes turned quite a few young men's heads. Her shapely figure had landed her several jobs doing runway modeling. She was also a makeup model in a video for a top-of-the-line cosmetic company.

Renée almost never wore makeup; when she did, it was only eyeliner and lip gloss. Renée towered over her friends, especially when she wore heels. She liked the modeling and looked forward to her next video, but her focus was on final exams. She was easygoing and down-to-earth; looks were an asset to the beautiful person she was inside.

Renée got out of the shower, dried off, and dressed quickly. After slipping on a long flowered print dress, she brushed her teeth. Her head moved from side to side as she closely inspected herself. The imprint still appeared slightly on her face, and a pimple was starting to come up on her forehead.

"Damn it! Oh well, can't deal with this now," she said, shrugging her shoulders.

She threw her hair back, checked herself out in a long closet mirror, and looked at her watch as she put it on. "Only fifteen minutes to get there. I'll get something to eat at school." She put on her shoes, grabbed her books and car keys, and yelled to her roommates, "I'll see you guys later." She walked out the door without even seeing them.

CHAPTER 2

Roaf Meisner was sitting at a long table in a conference room in the South African Parliament building. He was meeting with the members of the Constitutional Transition Committee. He said, "Our lives depend on this constitution. It must be fair to all people of this country. We can't alienate any one group from becoming a part of this government and having a say in what transpires." Heat rushed to his head and his face began to redden. "That is not the principle of democracy. That is not what democracy is all about."

Meisner was a thin, white man in his early fifties. His full head of black hair appeared thicker with the narrow features of his face. He looked tired but not worn, and he was still pleased with the accomplishment of the democratic all-race elections. And what an accomplishment it was; after centuries of segregation and dehumanization, they had implemented the creation of a unified government in South Africa.

Meisner was the previous government's chief negotiator in forging the new constitution. He could definitely understand the committee's concerns. His perturbed tone resonated throughout the room as he spoke to the members of the Constitutional Transition Committee. The men were newly elected officials of the first democratic government of South Africa. They needed the finalized constitution as soon as possible, preferably before they were to officially take their seats in the South African Democratic Parliament.

Meisner continued, "I know that we have not fully addressed the grievances of those groups that still oppose the transition, but we must finish *this* first." His thin fingers pointed to the thick book of papers in front of him. "The inauguration is coming in three weeks." The men nodded simultaneously.

There had been—and continued to be—destruction and civil unrest throughout the country. Those who opposed the democratic reform massacred innocent men, women, and children in the streets.

Black South Africans had never had any representation in the South African Parliament before the elections, even though they were three-fourths of the population. Apartheid was over! And for many, this was a threat. It meant a loss of power. It meant facing fears of retaliation because of past-legalized atrocities. It meant having to follow the lead of a man who, because of his skin color, as *they* had been brainwashed, was considered inferior to racist white South Afrikaans. It meant that black South African tribes would lose their homelands that had been designated by the rules of apartheid. It meant that the leaders of those tribes would lose their leadership. It meant that many people would have to change their thinking, their lives. It was change for the better, but people who are comfortable usually shun any type of change. Change makes people feel like they are losing control of what they thought was the only way.

Meisner said, "Those who opposed the movement of South Africa to democracy are fighting the change, and they are willing to die to stay the same."

Prior to the democratic elections of 1993, the bustling, modern city of Pretoria had been the seat of a South African Parliament that ruthlessly enforced apartheid to ensure the privilege and advantage of the white minority. There were three racially segregated houses of the South African Parliament—the House of Assembly for whites (who held the most power), the House of Representatives for mixed-race individuals, and the House of Delegates for East Indians. There was no House for Black South Africans.

Men of all colors sat at the table of the Constitutional Transitional Committee. They had attempted to bring all political parties and points of view into the democratization process, but they had failed to obtain 100 percent participation. The opposition still weighed heavily on their minds. Memories of death and destruction engulfed them in their victory.

CHAPTER 3

As he spoke to the committee, Roaf Meisner cited another story of violence and senseless killing, which had appeared in the Cape Town newspapers and illustrated the fact that factions were still fighting each other.

Tom Pullman lived in a nice middle-class neighborhood in Cape Town. He was a manager at a branch of one of the largest banks in South Africa. Tom had been married to his wife and college sweetheart for twenty-four years. They had one child, a daughter named Patricia.

Tom thought it was about time to have a heart-to-heart talk with his twenty-two-year old daughter. Patty had just graduated from college and definitely had her fill of life experiences. She had held several job positions while in high school and in college. While in high school, she'd worked in a clothing store as a sales clerk, at a theater as an usher and ticket salesperson, and in a dental office as a file clerk. She still found time to be a cheerleader at the high school soccer games and played on the girls' volleyball team.

In college, Patty had kept up her ambitious ways, working for a telemarketing company and volunteering at the university hospital. She graduated from college with honors, earning a degree in communications.

Tom thought she should be making some serious plans for her career. "Patty, let's go down to Dundee's Pub to have a beer. I want to talk to you," Tom yelled to his daughter who was in her room. *She's a good kid. She's really got a good head on her shoulders.* Tom gave himself a subliminal pat on the back for raising her well.

Patty said, "Okay, Dad. Sounds like a plan." She grabbed her purse and walked toward the door.

Patty and Tom turned and yelled "good-bye to Mrs. Pullman in the kitchen.

Dundee's was only three blocks down the street in a quiet suburb of Cape Town, a beautiful port city at the southern tip of the country. The city had remained fairly free of the violent wars that gripped South Africa before the first all-race elections.

Tom and Patty arrived at Dundee's pub and went inside.

"Tom, Patty, have a seat!" Dundee said as they entered. They were frequent patrons at this neighborhood hangout. Other people inside greeted them warmly.

Dundee was a tall, muscular thirty-eight-year-old white Afrikaner with sandy blond hair. He smiled as he approached the Pullmans. "What'll you have?" he said with a strong Afrikaner accent.

Tom smiled and replied, "We're gonna have a seat over there. We have to talk. We'll take two Heinekens."

After speaking to several people they knew, they took a seat in the corner near the entrance.

"Patty, what are your plans now that you've finished school?" Tom asked as Dundee set their beers down and went back to the bar.

Patty had a smirk, and she kind of smiled. "I knew you were going to ask me that!" She lifted her mug and took a sip of her beer. "To tell you the truth, Dad, I'm thinking about continuing my education and getting a hotel management certificate. You get to meet people from all over the world, and there are opportunities to travel and stay in affiliated hotels for free. I've been seriously considering it. I've even requested catalogues from the various schools that specialize"—Patty paused for a moment and looked toward the door—"in hotel management."

Five black South African men in trench coats entered the pub while she was talking. Something seemed peculiar—not that they were black South Africans—but they just stood in the doorway when it was 100 degrees outside. The pub was filled with young, white college students enjoying the beginning of the weekend.

The black men surveyed the scene, and the patrons looked up from their conversations. Everything seemed to happen in slow motion. One of the men at the door opened his coat and lifted a grenade-launching rifle and fired a nail-studded grenade into the middle of the pub.

Tom's eyes widened, and the only thing he knew to do was grab his daughter to cover her from the unavoidable attack.

Patty's screams were muffled under her father's arms.

The grenade did not explode, but as soon as it landed on the floor, the other men raised assault weapons from under their coats and opened fire on the crowd. People began to dive for cover, overturning tables and crawling along the floor to get away from the spray of bullets.

Many of the patrons were struck. Men and women were screaming in pain.

The gunmen continued to fire into the beleaguered crowd for a couple of minutes. When their clips were almost empty, they ran out of the pub, shooting at people on the street as they fled. They left a mass of wounded and dead on the sidewalk and inside the pub. In the pub, Patty Pullman was dead, and Tom was wounded and sobbing.

After he finished the story, Roaf Meisner looked at his fellow committee members. His eyes watered, and he said, "We must bring all South Africans to the table to stop this senseless bloodshed."

CHAPTER 4

Many attempts to bring all political parties and points of view into the democratization process had failed to obtain 100 percent participation. This was perhaps the greatest concern of the newly elected administration.

President-elect Nelson Mandela, President Botha, the Inkatha Freedom Party head, and representatives of many Afrikaner groups and other parties had held many meetings to find common ground that all could agree on to move the new democratic government forward peacefully.

Inkatha Zulus massacred Xhosas and other Zulus who were sympathetic to the ANC political causes. ANC Zulus retaliated and massacred Inkatha Zulus. The country was very unstable.

The Inkatha Freedom Party, conservatives, and other right-wing Afrikaner groups joined together to oppose the new order. They called themselves the Freedom Alliance.

Fighting, killings, protests, and saber-rattling continued to be the order of the day in South Africa. Prior to the elections, conservative white right-wingers repeatedly bombed several ANC campaign headquarters and the homes of ANC leaders and organizers, took over towns in Transvaal, Orange Free State, and Northern Natal to push their demand for an Afrikaner homeland, and boycotted the elections to continue their protests.

Nevertheless, Roaf Meisner, R. R. Nbutala, and the other participants in the writing of the constitution continued working on the final draft of the constitution that would be ratified with new amendments in the new Parliament. They had to move forward and continue the process.

The government had to address the grievances of those who rebelled against a democratic South Africa, but the transition had to be completed first. Once ratified, the constitution would be used to guide the new government for the next five years, after which, a new permanent constitution would be put in place. The constitution created nine new provinces, much like the states of the United States, with their own capitals and elected governments to run provincial affairs. The provinces would send representatives to the central government of Parliament, which ultimately governed all of South Africa, much like the federal government in Washington.

After the formal discussions about the new constitution, the topic turned to the upcoming event of the newly elected government. Heads of state and dignitaries from all over the world would attend the inauguration of the new president. Everyone who was anyone in South Africa from the world of politics, business, entertainment, or the arts had an invitation to the many balls or was clamoring to get one.

"I am sure you all have reserved this Friday for the Parliamentary Reception and three weeks from then for the Presidential Inauguration and Ball," Nbutala said. "So, therefore, I am sure we will not be meeting but once more this week."

Everyone nodded in agreement.

"If you haven't chartered a limousine by now, I am afraid it's too late. I called the Supreme Limousine Service because all government limousines are being used for foreign dignitaries, and I was unable to obtain one. I also had my secretary call all the other limousine services. All of them had their limousines reserved. I called my friend Roaf Meisner and told him of my plight, and he graciously invited my wife and me to ride with him."

Reserved laughter filled the room.

Meisner gathered his papers, stood up, and said, "If you do not have a limousine, I would suggest calling your friends and offering to bring champagne for the host and hostess as Mr. Nbutala did."

The meeting adjourned amidst an exchange of laughter and chatter as the participants discussed the upcoming events.

CHAPTER 5

Horace L. Davis sat back in his chair and closed his eyes for a minute. He had just finished another busy day at the US embassy in South Africa. Horace's new position was pretty exciting, and he was quite proud to be making history. These previous few months in South Africa had been dangerous and challenging with the campaign, the election, and the resistance.

Horace buzzed John Douglas and asked him to come to his office to go over preparations for the events of the next few weeks. While he waited for John to come in and update him, he reflected on his past few months.

The United States was the primary country pushing for the end of apartheid with sanctions and diplomacy, and Horace was responsible for articulating his government's position in these matters. US President Benson had made it quite clear that he and the world community expected the campaign to be fair and the election to be monitored to ensure that it was conducted properly and equitably. Nelson Mandela had been elected as expected and his party, the ANC, had captured most of the seats in Parliament, along with control of most of the nine provinces throughout South Africa. The inaugural proceedings that were set to occur in the next few days would be very important, and arrangements had to be made for the many US political dignitaries who would be attending.

Vice President Alvin B. Hunt was going to attend, and his advance people had been in Pretoria for a week already, making the necessary arrangements.

I need to get this briefing from John even though I know he's on top of it. I'm in the middle of this hubbub with my staff.

John Douglas entered Horace's office while he was still in deep thought. John was attaché to the South African embassy. "Horace, don't worry, we've made all the necessary arrangements and touched all the bases. The vice president's visit will go off like clockwork. All the brass will be taken care of, including your boss, Secretary Walter Christian, so quit worrying."

Handpicked by Horace, John had served as his attaché since President Tatum had appointed Horace ambassador to Haiti in 1985. Before that, John had been his chief administrator at a Washington law firm for twelve years. They went way back, and Horace knew that John was very sharp and efficient in carrying out his orders.

John said, "Everything will go as planned. I assure you."

"I know, I know. I trust you. I just don't want anything to go wrong." Horace looked at John and thought about all they'd been through together in the past fifteen years. "We still have all those white conservative fanatics and anti-ANC Zulu fanatics out there who would like to disrupt this whole thing. I don't know how you could be so assured even if we have everything in place. Just double-check everything—and triple-check security. I know it's the responsibility of the US Secret Service and the South African Secret Police, but I don't want anyone to get hurt, including myself."

"Okay. I'll double- and triple-check until they think I'm a fanatic myself. I'll stay on top of things until all these people have come and gone." John walked out of the office.

Horace knew that he really didn't have to worry; John Douglas was the best and had his back.

Horace reached for the phone and picked up the receiver. He decided to call his wife to tell her he would be late for dinner. They usually ate dinner together to make sure they spent some time together before going to bed. Lately, they'd both been so busy that it was difficult to keep to their commitment.

The telephones in the embassy living quarters rang several times before Sobrina answered. Sobrina, the head housekeeper, was a black South African woman in her early forties. A member of the Xhosa tribe, she had worked for the previous ambassador and had been in the employ of the US embassy for fourteen years. She was the no-nonsense director of the embassy staff. "Hello, this is the residence of the US ambassador, Horace Davis. May I help you," she said with a strong South African accent.

"Sobrina, this is Ambassador Davis. Tell Mrs. Davis that I am going to be a little late for dinner."

"Oh, sir, she was just asking about your presence. We are ready to serve dinner, you know," Sobrina said.

"Tell Mrs. Davis that I am still tied up here in the office. I will be up for dinner in a couple of hours. I hope she can wait."

"Yes, sir. We will hold back dinner, and I will give her the message," Sobrina replied.

Horace hung up the telephone, sat in his large, comfortable chair, and thought about the memories he shared with his wife. They had been together for twenty-five years.

At forty-five, Beverly Ann Scott-Davis still had soft tan skin. She had been a beauty when they met and fell in love at Howard University. As a first-year law school student, he had spotted the pretty junior coed with her sorority sisters on a Friday afternoon. He was staring at her so hard while he was walking with friends across the quad that he didn't see a bench in his path and fell right over it. All his buddies laughed at him, but he had to meet that girl.

They met shortly after that at a law school house party. No one at the university needed a formal invitation. If you heard about a party, you just went.

Horace saw Beverly dancing to a James Brown song with one of his friends. He asked the friend if he knew her, and he did. They had been in a class together when the friend was an undergrad.

Horace said, "Dude, you have to introduce me." After the introduction, Horace asked her to dance—and he didn't allow anyone else to dance with her for the rest of the night. They danced, laughed, and talked.

At the end of the party, Horace offered to take her home, but she declined. She would return home with her friends, but she gave Horace her telephone number and said, "Call me."

When Horace called the next day, they talked for hours. Beverly told Horace that she had recently broken up with her boyfriend and was not interested in a relationship, but they could be friends.

Horace said, "Okay." He knew his objective was to win over Beverly Scott and change her mind. He had found his love. They dated, and Horace soon won her over. They became inseparable and had a whirlwind romance. They were in love.

Horace had gone to high school in Washington and attended Georgetown University. He was six-two and 190 pounds and had played basketball while he studied international history and societies. After getting a BA in history, he attended Howard University's Law School and specialized in International Law.

Horace had grown up in the northwest section of Washington. His parents were upper-middle class and were in the mix with other educated blacks in the city. His father, a Baptist minister at one of the largest churches in Washington, was a staunch disciplinarian who insisted on a college education for all his children. He really didn't give his kids a choice—except for maybe which school they could attend. Horace's mother was a schoolteacher.

Beverly's parents had both finished at Howard University and lived in Bethesda, Maryland. Her father was a physician, and her mother an accountant. They, too, were in Washington's black upper-middle-class social mixers. Horace and Beverly's parents knew each other, but Beverly and Horace had never met while they were growing up. When Horace and Beverly met each other's parents, they realized that the parents knew each other and had mutual friends.

They got married as soon as Horace finished law school. Beverly had already graduated from Howard and was in graduate school at George Washington University. Horace and Beverly studied together while they were dating.

One night as they were taking a study break at the Jefferson Memorial, Horace got serious, knelt down in front of Beverly, presented her with a beautiful engagement ring, and asked her to marry him. She said yes!

Beverly's parents invited all of DC high society to the wedding. Beverly and Horace invited their friends. At the beautiful wedding, Horace and Beverly looked out over the attendees and said, "Who are all these people?" There were more than six hundred people in attendance. They had a great reception at the Hilton, and there were so many gifts that they had to store them in their parents' garages.

After getting her master's degree in sociology, Bev found a teaching position at Banneker High School in Washington.

After finishing law school, Horace joined a prestigious law firm that represented foreign governments' interests and international corporations. He worked his way up to partner with eighty- and ninety-hour workweeks for six or seven years. Two years into the marriage, their son, Darrell, was born. Three years later, Renée arrived. Horace settled back to fifty- and sixty-hour workweeks after Beverly began to complain about his lack of time around the house.

They worked very hard and saved. They bought a lovely, spacious home in the upper northwest Sixteenth Street area of Washington and began to travel in the circles of other well-educated movers and shakers in the area.

Horace and Beverly attended parties, banquets, fundraisers, and other events and moved up the corporate and social ladders. At law firm parties, they would mix with the partners, congressmen, important lobbyists, White House staffers, and so on. In the Democratic Black Caucus, almost every important representative hosted a party. There were parties at the White House when they were lucky enough to get an invitation—and many other embassy events.

Horace was respected in Washington's government circles, and the State Department called on him to make several goodwill trips. Finally, in 1985, President Tatum appointed Horace Ambassador to Haiti. He served in that capacity for three years, and then returned to his firm in Washington.

In 1989, President Benson wanted to assign an ambassador to South Africa who reflected the inevitable direction the president of the United States needed to take in light of the South African thrust toward abolishing apartheid. He appointed Horace Davis as the US ambassador to South Africa.

Horace arrived in South Africa and was immediately immersed in the country's movement toward freedom. He met with the South African white government officials, including President F. W. de Klerk, to share the message of the position of the US government on the abolition of apartheid. He met with the ANC leadership, including Nelson Mandela, to share the same messages. He also met with any other factions that would meet with him. He kept the State Department informed of his activities. He was a very busy ambassador. Shortly after his arrival in South Africa, the ANC was unbanned, apartheid ended, and Nelson Mandela was set free.

CHAPTER 6

On a platform, Verdi Piethro Higgs was addressing more than two thousand white members of the Freedom Alliance. He was wearing an all-black military uniform with swastikas on his sleeves. He was a white supremacist in his middle thirties. He was only five feet seven and 160 pounds, but he was a fiery orator like his hero, Adolf Hitler. The crowd was cheering at his remarks. The Freedom Alliance was an unlikely coalition of Zulu nationalists, white separatists, and conservative black homeland leaders. They had not done well in the election and were on the outside looking in.

Higgs was president of the Organization for the Preservation of White Rights. Headlines of all major newspapers around the world had announced that apartheid had ended. Though it had been devastating to 85 percent of the black South African population, it gave the 7 percent white population a great advantage and protection against fair competition. The Freedom Alliance did not want it to end. The election had been held, and they had lost.

Higgs said, "This is a travesty and is unacceptable. We must do whatever is necessary to defeat this illegitimate government."

All this would be lost unless they did something about the transition right away. Higgs had been a police sergeant in the Transvaal region. He had a reputation for being ruthless and brutal in his dealings with black South Africans. When it became clear to him that the end of apartheid was coming and Nelson Mandela would be elected president, he quit his job and began working for the Organization for the Preservation of White Rights (translated privilege). His organization was one of sixty Afrikaner conservative white right-wing organizations that opposed the end of apartheid and wanted a white homeland that would be separate from black-led South Africa. The Freedom Alliance had pledged to do anything necessary to have things their way even if it meant going to war against the newly elected South African government. The Volksfront could not agree on where this Volkstaat would be or who would govern; they just knew they wanted a white homeland.

Higgs continued with his speech while other white organization leaders stood behind him on the platform. "We made a gallant effort to disrupt these elections, but they brought in so many foreign supporters... especially those people from the United States. These Americans want to take over our economy and our farms with big farming conglomerates and take over our diamond and gold and other industries. These foreigners are now in bed with the communists who backed the ANC because they knew that once they were in power, they could take our land and our industries and control us. Our ancestors fought off these wild Zulus and the British and anybody who challenged them so that we could have a future in South Africa. We are not going to just give up our birthright without a fight."

The crowd responded with cheers and applause.

Higgs waited patiently for the cheering to subside. "We are not going to allow the white traitors, do-gooders, or foreign governments such as the United States or these ANC kaffirs to dictate to us how we must live our lives in South Africa. These kaffirs are going to treat us like they claim we have treated them in apartheid. This is our land! We are South Africans! We have been on this land for three hundred years! We will not be turned back from our demands for a Volkstaat! We must have a Volkstaat in order to survive in black-led South

Africa! Long live the Afrikaner Volksfront! Long live the Volkstaat!"
Higgs, stiff with resentment, hatred, and loyalty to his own kind,
raised his right arm in the air in a manner resembling a Nazi salute.
The crowd followed his gesture as though puppets on the
same string and began to shout, "Long live Volksfront! Long live
Volkstaat! Long live Volksfront! Long live Volkstaat!" They chanted
hypnotically for almost ten minutes.

Higgs turned to the organization leaders on the platform, shook
some hands, and then signaled to his top associates and left the
platform. The crowd began to disperse, and Higgs went into one of
the nearby houses, which was the Volksfront headquarters. After
the rally, he was slated to make a presentation to the organization's
leaders. They would all meet in the large conference room.

The Volksfront headquarters was located in the Orange Free
State near the Transvaal region. The rural farming area was settled
by Afrikaners who were descendants of the Dutch settlers who came
to South Africa in the 1700s and became known as the Boers. This
area was the most ultraconservative, right wing part of South Africa.

When most of the Volksfront organization leaders were
assembled in the room, Higgs said, "Esteemed members of the
Volksfront. I have asked you to meet with me today in order to
present to you a plan to give us leverage in our struggle for a Volkstaat.
It is well known that the most powerful ally of this new black South
African government is the United States of America, especially since
the election of President Benson. He has endorsed Mandela from the
very beginning of his administration. He has promoted sanctions
and boycotts against white South Africa to force us to change our
political system. The US ambassador to South Africa carries out his
wishes and the wishes of the American State Department daily. The
black ambassador pushes very hard to make South Africa change and
conform to the wishes of the black South African ANC leadership.

The greatest leverage we have is to embarrass Mandela and his new government by striking at the government of the United States from here in South Africa. This will show Washington that we do not want its interference and will show that Mandela doesn't have his hand fully grasped around South Africa. It will give us leverage to negotiate for a white homeland, a Volkstaat. What I am proposing cannot be discussed even in this meeting. I will present my plan only to the governing council when they meet in two days. Expect a bold and daring action, and have the courage to allow us to carry it out."

Higgs thanked the gathering, turned, and left the room. His entourage, which was made up of the staunchest haters of black South Africans, followed him. They were all white supremacists. They were ex-policemen who had quit the South African Police Force after the election. They were ex-soldiers who had fought against the ANC and the Inkatha Freedom Party and lost relatives and comrades in the battles. They loved, obeyed, and followed their leader because he could articulate their feelings and passion. These men and women did not want to be part of a united, all-race South Africa.

CHAPTER 7

Musa Goba was speaking to the Council of Elders. "My Zulu brothers, I come before you to speak of grave circumstances. This meeting was called because, even though we made every effort to thwart the election of the Xhosa tribesman and ANC pig, Nelson Mandela, he was still elected, and the ANC now controls the politics of South Africa. There was tremendous interference, as we all know, from the West, especially from the United States of America, and our archenemy, the ANC, is now in power, and the new constitution has been ratified. We boycotted the election. We fought against this election, and now we must deal with the reality of this election. We are still not into the fold, and we must let Pretoria know that we will not be brought into the fold without tremendous compromise on their part in the granting to us of a Zulu homeland in Natal, our ancestral Kwazulu homeland. Our ancestors left Kwazulu to the Zulu people. Our forefathers gave us a mandate and a responsibility to maintain Kwazulu as the home of the Zulu people. We cannot relinquish this land under any circumstances, even if we have to enter into civil war with this ANC government and South Africa."

Kwazulu, a homeland area in the Natal region of South Africa located in the eastern shore area, is the home of most of the Zulu people. The area is steeped in ancient tradition, and many of the Zulu practices have been preserved by Zulu inhabitants through the centuries.

Musa Goba was the chief and powerful political leader of the eight million Zulus. Goba and the other Zulu leaders were quite concerned with their role in the new government. Apartheid had given Musa Goba his power over Kwazulu and the Zulu people of the Natal Province. Through the creation of homelands by the white apartheid system, black homeland presidents had almost dictatorial powers in their homelands.

Goba was meeting with the Zulu Council of Elders as well as black homeland leaders to discuss their reactions to the newly elected government and the new constitution, which called for the dismantling of all homelands and the creation of nine provincial areas. The enforcement of this new constitution was of grave concern and had to be dealt with immediately.

The meeting place was a small wood-framed building in the village of Zowanda in Kwazulu. Ten to twelve men, most of them elderly, were discussing the election around a long wooden table, including Goba, Gotha Bathalers, assistant chief of the Zulu, Goodwyn Zwelthana, king of the Zulu, Welton Betelema, chief of staff of the Zulu military forces, and leaders in the Natal Province area.

Goba continued, "We have entered into a strange, distasteful alliance with the white racist Boermen in order to find some avenue to stop this debacle and to be sure that we retain the sovereignty that we have fought for and wanted for so many years in South Africa. We want our home rule! We want our homeland! We want our autonomy! And we do not want to be a part of this ANC government, this government of our enemies! We must act, even though it may call for drastic measures in order for us to continue our Zulu way of life."

When he completed his presentation to the Council of Elders and chiefs of the homelands, Goba sat down and looked sternly at each man. Immediately, Welton Betelema got to his feet. Goba noticed that he appeared to be agitated and waited for him to speak.

Betelema said, "We, as the military arm of the Zulu, are prepared, if necessary, to wage guerrilla warfare and to fight as we have in the past for our freedom, and for our autonomy, and for our self-rule, and for our secession from this South African government." He pounded his fist into his other hand. "We will do whatever the elders tell us to do in order to preserve Kwazulu, and to preserve our king, and to preserve our chief, and preserve this austere Council of Elders and chiefs of the homelands! We will do whatever you command us to do!"

The elders nodded in agreement.

Goba again rose to his feet. "With the election, Mandela now has the ANC militia and the entire military might of South Africa at his disposal. We, therefore, cannot commit our forces directly against this government as we have in the past against the ANC. It is necessary for the Zulu to join forces with the white Afrikaners because they want a white homeland with autonomy. We have no problem with that as long as they stay in the Orange Free State and we have Kwazulu in Natal. We can trade with them. We can do whatever is necessary to get along with the so-called Volkstaat as long as we are equals. If we go to war, to secede, we will have to fight by the Afrikaners' sides. I believe that we will have to go to the Zulu people to determine if we can fight alongside the Afrikaners."

With that said, the elders and homeland leaders discussed the proposals that had been presented and decided to go back to their respective towns and villages to talk with their councils to find out what the Zulu people wanted to do.

Goba said, "Before we decide that it is necessary to wage war against the new South African government, we must devise a plan that will force Mandela and his Parliament to make deep compromises in the constitution, compromises that will grant Kwazulu autonomy and the right to choose our own leaders."

King Zwelthana interjected, "I will call for a meeting with Mandela and demand sovereignty in Kwazulu."

The elders and homeland leaders agreed to this plan.

Betelema leaped to his feet and shouted, "We cannot go to this Xhosa pig and beg him for our land; we must use a more direct assault to force him to amend the constitution to give us Kwazulu as a separate nation."

Gotha Bathalens said, "Welton, we must first try to keep the lines of communication open. We must meet with Mandela and let him know that our demands, which were made before the election, have not changed. We allowed the election to go forward with the assurance that an outside United Nations mediator would meet with both sides to find a compromise area of agreement for the Inkatha Freedom Party and for the Freedom Alliance. We must give this process a chance. With war, many Zulu tribesmen will die. This may not be necessary to get what we want."

The entire group appeared to agree.

Betelema whispered, "Goba, the Zulu people and the Inkatha Freedom Party need more leverage before going to Mandela to demand autonomy for Kwazulu, but I will follow the wishes of the council."

The meeting ended with a resolution to have King Zwelthana and Musa Goba meet with President Mandela to present the Zulu demands.

Betema stormed out of the meeting. He was very upset with the outcome and was not in agreement.

CHAPTER 8

Renée arrived at UCLA at eight thirty. She was late, but her study buddies were also late some mornings. Renée was a bit stressed out because she hated to be late; her parents had always taught her to be punctual and to not make people wait for her. She parked in Lot 9 and hurried past the residence halls. She passed the frat houses on Veteran Avenue, went through the tunnel past the bookstore in the student union building, and went up the hill to the quad. She continued past the classroom buildings to the main library.

As she was walking, Renée thought, *Just two more days and three finals. This year has been tough, but it's almost over. Thank God. I have to get packed because we're leaving early Friday morning. It's going to be great to see Mom and Dad. It's going to be a great summer!*

She was looking forward to summer vacation in South Africa with her parents. She had invited three of her college friends to stay with them for a month in Pretoria. They were all excited about being in post-apartheid South Africa with its changes and danger. It would be a great adventure. They were planning to travel all over South Africa, with escorts because of the unrest. They wanted to see it all and be a part of this newly democratic nation. It was very exciting, but she had to focus on finishing her final exams.

The four students in her microbiology study group were waiting on the library steps. She said, "Hi, you guys. Sorry I'm late. I'm just moving slow this morning."

Brad said, "Don't worry about it. We've all been late before, and most of us didn't get here more than two minutes ago. I don't feel like going into the library today. I am so damned tired of this place that I just can't go in there."

Brad Jones, a small black guy about five feet six and 135 pounds, was from Detroit. He wore his hair in short dreads on the top half of his head and very closely cut on the sides. His horn-rimmed, small, round sunglasses made him appear deep, and he was. Brad was a biology major who "loved" biology. He was an egghead—sort of nerdy, but cool.

"I hear you. Let's go find a table by the student union building. This is a gorgeous day. We can study outside. Just concentrate on the books, Ali, and stop looking at all the girls' butts," Tina replied. As everybody laughed, she added, "Just kidding, Ali, just kidding!"

Tina Johnson was a pretty, light-skinned black girl about five feet five with an hourglass figure. Tina was Renée's best friend. Her father was an architect. She wanted to be a psychiatrist like her mother. Tina had features that made her appear Asian and black, but her parents were both black. She worked at modeling jobs, sold cosmetics in upscale department stores, and worked as an extra in music videos and movies.

Ali didn't say anything to Tina; he just smiled. All of his friends knew he liked the ladies, and they liked him.

Ali Abijan was a tall, well-built Persian hunk. He had olive skin, large dark brown eyes, and lots of long hair. He wanted to be an actor, but he was taking microbiology as part of his biology major. He wanted to get a lab tech certificate so that he could work until he got his big acting break.

Michelle Nguyen, a tall, slender Asian girl, was working her way through school as a part-time model and sales girl in department stores. Her parents had fled Vietnam at the end of the war. She was born in the United States and was very American in her views. She was premed, studied hard, and was a good student. She echoed her friends' desire to study outside rather than in the library.

They walked back down the hill to the tables near the student union building. It was a beautiful day. The temperature was about seventy-five degrees, the cloudless skies were blue, and there was a gentle breeze. It was a typical Southern California spring day. There were other students studying outside the student union building, and they were lucky to find a table that had just been vacated. When they began to study, they made sure that everyone stayed focused. After about an hour and a half, they decided to take a break. Renée, Tina, and Michelle walked over to the water fountain.

"Have you guys started packing yet?" Renée asked. "I haven't packed a thing!"

Tina replied, "Who has time to pack? I'm lucky if I can get two or three hours of sleep. I'm just going to have to pull an all-nighter packing. I hope I have time to do some shopping. I need to buy some things before I pack."

"I've packed a few things, but I'm nowhere near finished," Michelle said. "Plus, I'm still getting things straight at work so that I can return to my job. Has anyone talked to Denise?"

"Yeah, I talked to her last night. She'll be finished Thursday morning, and she'll have time to pack and get ready to go," Renée answered.

The guys called to them; it was time to get back to studying.

Denise Ortega was majoring in political science and ultimately wanted to be a lawyer. She was a third-generation Mexican American. Her poor grandfather had come from Mexico with a dream. He had left the family farm in Jalisco and moved to the hustle and bustle of nearby Mexico City. He learned to cook in hotel kitchens and eventually became the manager of the culinary department of one of the large hotels in which he worked.

Mr. Ortega decided to move his young family to Los Angeles for more opportunities. He started a small restaurant named Ortega's. The restaurant was a success, and his sons, daughter, and wife worked in the business. Denise's father and his brothers and sisters opened six other restaurants that were all very successful. Denise and her two older brothers had decided not to go into the restaurant business.

Renée and her friends had taken a course on the emergence of democracy in South Africa in the Afro-American Studies Department. After the course, Renée invited her friends, who had lived in the same dorm with her in their freshman year, to come home with her. The girls could barely contain their excitement.

Tina, Michelle, and Denise had a million questions they wanted to ask Renée about the plans, but they would have to wait until after the final exams. Studying for final exams was difficult, but they knew they had to focus. They just wanted the exams to be over. They were going to attend the inauguration of President Mandela and meet all the important people in South African government and society, especially the young men. They were going to visit South Africa's beautiful modern cities, fantastic coastlines with breathtaking beaches and rock formations, great national parks, and wild game preserves. They were going to meet people of all races. If South Africa was successful in making the transition from apartheid to democracy, it was going to be one of the greatest countries in the world. They were looking forward to their vacation, but they had to finish their finals first.

CHAPTER 9

Goba and his entourage arrived first for a meeting of the Freedom Alliance.

The meeting place for the Freedom Alliance was a compromise between the mostly white area of the Orange Free State and the Zulu homeland of rural Natal. It had once been an Inkatha guerrilla campsite with thatch huts shaped like beehives and dried straw on the roofs and outdoor fireplaces. There were about eight huts for living quarters and two larger huts for meetings and administration. However, they abandoned the camp when it became too vulnerable to attacks by the ANC and the Volksfront.

Goba had sent an advance party to prepare for this secret assembly. They had set up tables and chairs in the largest building at the campsite. The building did not have sides, but the thatched roof was connected to poles on a platform. The building had been swept and cleaned, and food had been prepared for the meeting. His advance team had brought rice and beans, curry chicken, green beans, grilled beefsteaks, and bread. They had prepared rice pudding for dessert. They brought beer and fresh cold water. All this was in preparation for the conclave with Higgs and his entourage to discuss the strategy of the Freedom Alliance to resist and sabotage the new government.

There was no love lost between the two groups. In fact, they deeply hated and distrusted each other. However, the prospect of a new democratic government led by the ANC brought them together for this clandestine meeting. The unlikely allies were strange bedfellows indeed!

Betelema, commander of the Inkatha guerrilla forces, did not trust the Afrikaners or their intentions. As a precaution, just in case something went wrong with the meeting, he placed about two dozen troops within a quarter mile of the campsite. He also placed camouflaged snipers in several trees around the campsite, and there were sentries with radios every mile starting five miles from the campsite to monitor the progress of the Higgs entourage.

Higgs and his entourage made their appearance as scheduled. His motorcade came up the mountain and was spotted by the advance sentries half an hour before he and his party arrived in the camp. Higgs and the Volksfront followers were nervous and a bit on edge as they drove to the meeting. Higgs did not trust them. They had been at war with each other for years, but they both needed an ally to carry out the plans for armed resistance against the new government. Their coalition would be large enough, strong enough and equipped enough to wage a civil war against the ANC and South African government troops.

Goba stood with members of his party at the top of the platform. When Higgs arrived with his entourage, Goba felt a little apprehensive. He waited for Higgs to get out of his vehicle and ascend the stairs with his party. The two men greeted each other very stiffly.

"Welcome, Mr. Higgs. I trust your journey was not a difficult one," Goba said.

Higgs replied, "No, it was not, Mr. Goba. I hope that you are in good health."

The leaders shook hands while other members of the two parties looked on.

Goba said, "We have drinks and food and restroom facilities to refresh you after your long journey. Then we may begin the meeting." Higgs and his party were hot and thirsty and accepted the offer. Goba and his group had already refreshed themselves and waited patiently with their drinks on one side of the table.

Goba and Higgs had met the year before at a meeting they had attended at the South African Parliament with influential groups in South African politics. They, along with most of the homeland presidents, had been dissenters in the constitutional talks being held primarily between President de Klerk and Nelson Mandela. They felt that they had not only been ignored in the process—but had the most to lose. Their strategy had failed to place a hold on the democratic reconstruction of the South African government. However, as a unified force, Higgs and Goba believed they would have more power to convince the new government to grant them sovereignty.

They sat at the table and faced each other. It was the fourth meeting between the two men since the formation of the Freedom Alliance. The first meeting had been tense and challenging, and the distrust in the room was palpable. However, subsequent meetings eased the tension somewhat. Many plans and strategies had been formulated and followed, but the election campaigns and the election process continued.

Goba said, "In spite of all the planning and disruption and upheavals that we have created in South Africa, the election process continued and gained momentum. The Inkatha Zulu have been in a state of war against the ANC for years, and our efforts have increased since 1991, yet it seems inevitable that Nelson Mandela and his party will demand that we give up our power in our homelands. We cannot live with this! As you know, Mr. Higgs, our killings and sieges, your bombings and massacres, and even the clandestine training and arming of our guerrillas by the South African police did not stop de Klerk and Mandela. Now that Mandela has been elected and his party is controlling Parliament, we must decide whether to negotiate or fight. We may also choose to negotiate while we prepare to fight."

Higgs listened patiently for his unlikely ally to finish. "We Afrikaners are prepared to fight and die, if necessary, to secure our Volkstaat in Orange Free State. We are willing to negotiate to gain time, but now we are negotiating from a weak position. Mandela now has all the power in his hands. We must find some way to turn the tables and gain some leverage for negotiating if we are to successfully reach our goals of autonomous states."

Betelema, seated next to Goba, leaned over and whispered in his ear.

Goba listened closely and then said, "The Americans, through their ambassador, have behind the scenes been most influential in persuading the white government of South Africa to dismantle apartheid. I have been informed by my security chief, who has an informant in Parliament and one stationed at the US embassy, that the US ambassador's daughter and her friends will be coming to South Africa for a visit in the next few days. This information may be useful in determining a strategy for more leverage."

Higgs listened thoughtfully and then replied, "If I am following your train of thought, Mr. Goba, I believe we could come up with a plan to somehow use this information to our advantage. The Americans would be reluctant to support a black government that had terrorists, excuse me, freedom fighters in its midst that would harm Americans. Look how they handled Somalia."

Goba paused and then replied, "I believe that we should now devise a plan and take it to our councils to discuss and approve or disapprove what we present. We should not act hastily because we do not want to incur the wrath of the American government unnecessarily."

The entire group began discussing all the possibilities of a plan with the new information about the US ambassador's daughter. The plan Musa Goba brought back to the Zulu Council of Elders was to kidnap the American ambassador's daughter and her friends. The plan was very risky because Mandela and de Klerk would have to react to this provocative event to save the pride of the South African government. They would probably send the army against any parties that carried out such a plot. If the plan worked, it would probably be a short-term gain because after they got the girls back, they would retaliate. The US government would probably send troops into South Africa to support the South African Army. None of the scenarios that were presented were good as far as the Council of Elders could see, and after much discussion and deliberations, it was decided that the plan could backfire and cause them grave problems with the new government. It was too risky. Likewise, the Volksfront leaders decided that the plan had too many areas for failure and should be scrapped.

Higgs and Betelema vehemently disagreed and secretly met to streamline and finalize the plan to kidnap the ambassador's daughter and her friends.

Betelema and Higgs had a secret meeting at a rural house in Naboomspruit to discuss the necessary logistics for carrying out their plan.

Higgs said, "I will have my men in Angola board the flight when it leaves from the airport in Launda."

Betelema replied, "We will be waiting for you at the airfield here." He pointed to a map on a table. After more discussion and agreement, the men were determined to implement their plan.

CHAPTER 10

Beverly Davis had been preparing for the reception for at least a week. It was going to be the premier affair in a series of celebrations of the new democracy in South Africa. Important people from all over the country and all the embassies were coming to meet the Parliament. It was going to be the biggest ball before the inaugural festivities.

Horace was going to be the highest-ranking representative from the United States, and people would be scrutinizing their dress, conversation, and every move. Beverly and her assistants were making sure that the US embassy attendees looked the part and said the right things.

Horace had been so busy that he would never have time to take care of the most important protocol functions. Beverly had always been there for Horace, making sure everything was perfect when politically influential guests came into town. She was a loving wife, a fantastic mother, and she had assisted a great deal with Horace's political responsibilities as an ambassador.

Beverly was in the living quarters of the embassy. The luxurious living quarters included a living room, a formal dining room, a family room, four spacious bedrooms, a huge master bedroom, a kitchen, maid's quarters, two offices, and seven bathrooms.

Beverly was busier than ever with follow-up telephone calls to staff members. She was sitting on the comfortable chair behind her desk in her office, holding the telephone as her mind ran over all the things that had to be done before she and Horace left for the ball.

She called John Douglas and said, "I hope that you and Horace are planning to leave the office on time."

John assured her that they would leave on time, but Beverly decided to call the embassy staff manager. "Ann, be sure to call downstairs to remind the ambassador that he must stop his meetings by five o'clock. I told him before he left for the Parliament House to be finished and back here to get ready, but you know once he gets off into his meetings, he forgets all about the time."

"Okay, Mrs. Davis. I will make sure he gets that message."

Ann Brown was a career State Department employee who had been assigned to the South African embassy a few years before the appointment of Horace Davis. She was a short Xhosa woman who was thick and solid. Ann was setting out the clothes for Ambassador Davis and Mrs. Davis and giving instructions to the embassy staff. She was a stern manager of the household and its staff, a duty she'd had for twenty years in various embassies in South Africa.

As Mrs. Davis instructed, Ann selected a beautiful black embroidered gown from the walk-in closet. The long-sleeved gown had a low neckline that descended from the shoulders to form a curve similar to a lover's heart. The dress was elegant, sophisticated, and very sexy. Mrs. Davis was sure to get many compliments from the attendees of the ball. Ann put the dress on the bed and reached for the handsome black tuxedo that Mr. Davis would wear.

Ann placed Horace's tuxedo on the bed next to Beverly's dress then selected the shirt and bow tie that Mrs. Davis had chosen. The women inspected the wardrobes and nodded in satisfaction. With the clothes set and approved for the event, Ann left the room. The US ambassador and his lovely wife were going to be the handsome representatives of America. Beverly was still concerned that Horace would not make it back on time.

Horace finished his last meeting, signed his last document, and checked his watch. He remembered that Beverly, Ann, and John had reminded him to quit work early to make sure he had enough time to rest before getting ready for the reception. He sat back in his blue leather chair and thought about recent events in South Africa. He marveled over the fact that he and his wife were going to a reception for a democratically elected Parliament that all the people of South Africa had the opportunity to elect by their vote. What a monumental step for this country.

His watch read five fifteen. "Better hurry," he said to himself.

Horace chose the stairs over the elevator and ran up to the third floor. He was in good shape and barely broke a sweat. Horace was forty-eight years old and didn't look his age at all. He looked like he was still in his thirties. People were never able to guess his age unless they knew the ages of his daughter and son. From that information, they might be able to guess his age. When asked about his secret for staying young, he'd say, "Well, I still get out there with the young'uns and play a few pick-up games of basketball." He also went to the gym, pumped iron, and played tennis occasionally.

He hurried into the living quarters. When he entered their bedroom, Beverly and Ann looked at him with disapproving expressions and said, "You're late!"

Horace still had to shower, shave, and get dressed.

The reception was at seven o'clock, and Beverly and Horace took the elevator from their living quarters. Beverly was irritated by Horace's tardiness and was not speaking to him. He did not say a word about his day or anything else. He was going to allow her to cool off.

They walked out the front door at six thirty sharp. A chauffeured black Lincoln limousine was waiting for them in the courtyard with American flags on both sides of the front fenders. They hastily entered the limousine. It was almost a thirty-minute drive to the Parliament House.

Beverly's thoughts had been going a million miles a minute all day long. Had President Mandela's dinner been prepared properly? Had the limousines been rerouted away from the possible attacks by Zulus and white supremacists that opposed the election? The South African military had given notice that these precautions would need to be taken. Was the red carpet clean for the arrival of the guests? Had the announcer of the arriving guests gotten over his laryngitis or had they found a replacement? These things were not her responsibility, but she wanted everything to be perfect. As they got closer to the ballroom, she thought about Renée.

"Horace, do you realize that Renée will be home in just a couple of days? I can hardly wait to see my baby. I have all kinds of things planned for the girls. I have arranged for them to tour all of South Africa. They must have bodyguards wherever they go." She paused for a moment. "It's still dangerous out here. I have to talk to the general to make sure they will be safe wherever they venture. I am planning at least two parties so they can meet some of these influential people. There is real history going on here, and I want them to be a part of it." Coyly, Beverly smiled. "Not to mention meeting all the eligible young men that I will also be inviting to these parties."

Horace nodded.

Beverly's voice went up an octave. "I have had all the bedrooms prepared for Renée and her friends, and I've set up a shopping spree in Johannesburg. Oh, this is so exciting! And, of course, they are going to the presidential inauguration. Horace, is there anything else we can plan that I've left out?"

Horace started to answer but was interrupted by the chauffeur's announcement that they had arrived at the Parliament House. Horace and Beverly glanced out the tinted windows at the long line of limousines, and their demeanors changed immediately.

Beverly cupped her hands gently across her knees and stiffened her back. She looked at Horace to be certain that he looked perfect.

Horace straightened his tie and brushed his hands against his thighs to push out invisible wrinkles.

Beverly thought, *Horace's position as the first black US ambassador to South Africa has placed a considerable amount of pressure on us. Our every move, every word will be closely observed and scrutinized by the guests at the ball. We are representing the United States, and our personal concerns have to be postponed until later.*

The chauffeur opened the limousine door, and Beverly and Horace emerged, looking radiant and dignified. They ascended the Parliament House steps, glancing around to see who they could see and to see who was watching them.

When they entered the building, a beautiful black South African girl in an evening gown made with traditional South African colors met them. Her hair was short and natural, and her eyes were twinkling when she approached. "Good evening, Ambassador and Mrs. Davis. I am Sonya, your escort. Welcome to the Parliamentary reception. Please follow me."

Ambassador and Mrs. Davis followed the young lady to the ballroom and presented them to the official greeter, who promptly turned and announced, "United States Ambassador Horace L. Davis and Mrs. Beverly A. Davis."

Sonya escorted them into the ballroom and took their coats. "Ambassador Davis and Mrs. Davis, please ask for me when you are ready to leave. I will retrieve your coats and summon your limousine."

She turned and walked away rhythmically, as though she was dancing to the beat of a drum.

Horace and Beverly scanned the crowd. As they walked through the ballroom, they greeted many of the dignitaries.

D. W. Pietha, head of South African National Security was with his wife. He said, "Good evening, Ambassador and Mrs. Davis. I trust that you are well."

Mrs. Pietha smiled and nodded. They exchanged niceties and moved on. Horace spotted Ralston B. Oppenheimer, a member of a wealthy mining and manufacturing family, and Raymond Ndulata, security chief and director of the militia for the ANC. They were engaged in a light conversation, but they stopped when Beverly and Horace approached.

"Hello, Ambassador and Mrs. Davis. I'm very happy to see you," Mr. Ndulata said with a big smile.

"I am too," Mr. Oppenheimer said.

"This is a wonderful occasion. We are all optimistic that we can make this transition with a minimal amount of conflict," Horace replied. "The president of the United States and Congress are committed to supporting President Mandela and the new Parliament in its efforts to bring democracy, justice, and stability to South Africa. It is unfortunate that all parties and factions haven't chosen to participate in this historic transition." Horace shook his head. "However, the United States is hopeful that they will come to the table in good faith to peacefully work out their differences with the new government."

Mr. Ndulata said, "Those who have not accepted this change are continuing to threaten armed revolution and continuing their campaigns of violence and terror. Government security does not believe these threats are idle, given the recent history of violence in this country. People are not afraid of killing or dying for their causes.

In the past four years, more than fifteen thousand lives have been taken because of revolutionary violence. We believe this will continue and won't go away because of the magic wand of elections. We must be prepared and committed to repel those who would violently turn back our progress."

The official greeter announced, "Sir Garfield Thurman III and Mrs. Abigail Thurman."

Garfield Thurman was a career politician and had been chief of staff of de Klerk's presidential staff. As a member of the transition committee, Thurman was one of the chief negotiators with the ANC in dismantling apartheid.

The announcement gave Beverly the opportunity to break away from the conversation to say hello to the wife of the Canadian ambassador. Joann Morris and Beverly greeted each other as old friends, accepted wine from the waiters, and began to talk about things other than politics. Beverly was very excited about Renée's homecoming and wanted to talk to Joann about some of her plans.

Beverly was admiring her husband and the seemingly easy way he interacted with the attendees. She was no longer angry about his tardiness. Her thoughts drifted to Renée and her concern for Renée's safety while visiting South Africa. *I want them to have a great time, but most of all, I want them to be safe.*

Horace called her from across the room to greet someone.

CHAPTER 11

Finals were finally over, and Renée had just one day to pack. It had been a very hectic week, but she and the posse were ready to go. Bill, Denise's boyfriend, had borrowed his parents' jeep, and Andre, Renée's friend—nothing serious, just someone to go out with, see a movie, eat or just hang out—had a van, so they could caravan to the Tom Bradley International Terminal at LAX. Bill picked up Denise and Michelle and their suitcases. Andre packed up Tina and Renée's suitcases. They all were going to meet at Renée's apartment before catching their flight to New York. In Angola, they would change planes and complete their flight to Johannesburg. They would be flying for twenty-two hours, including stopovers in New York and Luanda.

Bill arrived at Renée's apartment with Denise and Michelle as Andre had just finished packing Tina and Renée's baggage into the jeep. Everyone was determined to be on time for the flight. The posse was usually late to everything, but this was the beginning of summer vacation, a fantastic adventure, and the start of an exciting chapter in their young lives.

Denise said, "All right, homeys. Let's get going."

Everybody laughed. The excitement showed in their every movement, their smiles, and their eyes. Even the boys were excited for their friends.

"Okay, you guys. Check everything. Nobody's forgotten anything, right?" Bill asked.

"Who has the tickets?" Tina asked.

"I do," said Renée.

They had decided that Renée should purchase the tickets since she was making the arrangements. Each of the girls had already paid her.

"Does everyone have their passport?" Renée asked.

Each girl checked again and answered in the affirmative.

"Baggage is packed. We have the passports and the tickets. Let's go!" Tina said. "Oh no. I forgot my carry-on bag; it's still upstairs. Renée, give me the keys." She grabbed the keys and bolted upstairs.

"She'd forget her head if it wasn't attached to her body," Michelle said.

They all laughed, got into the vehicles, and waited for Tina. She returned with her carry-on baggage and got into the van with Andre and Renée. They were ready for the trip to begin.

They arrived at the airport two hours before their flight was to depart to make sure that the baggage was checked in properly and routed all the way to Johannesburg. They did not want to deal with their luggage again until the journey was over. Everyone was excited and talked incessantly even though they were exhausted from studying.

Denise passionately kissed Bill good-bye as though she would never see him again.

"Goodness," said Michelle. "Come up for air so we don't miss the plane."

Everyone laughed. The girls hugged Bill and Andre and thanked them for being their chauffeurs for the day.

Andre kissed Renée good-bye as they hugged.

"I'll send you a postcard. Be back in about a month." Renée gave Andre another quick peck on the lips and turned to catch up with her friends. They were in line to board the flight to JFK. The girls found their seats together, put their carry-on luggage overhead, and settled in for the trip.

"Fasten your seatbelts," Denise said. Simultaneously, all of the girls followed her order.

They joked with one another and talked about missing their boyfriends. The airplane taxied down the runway and waited its turn for takeoff. The pilot came on the intercom and announced they were ready for takeoff and asked the flight attendants to take their seats. Once again, the plane taxied down the runway at greater and greater speeds until liftoff; they were airborne and on the way to New York!

The length of the flight, though very long and tiring, was not going to bother these excited young ladies because they were exhausted and planned to catch up on a lot of missed sleep. They continued to chatter excitedly for about an hour into the flight. They were fed breakfast and then quietly retreated into their own thoughts.

Renée said, "Please, God, watch over us so that we reach South Africa safely and have a wonderful and fun vacation."

One by one, they fell asleep, each looking forward to their summertime adventure.

CHAPTER 12

The four white Afrikaner men in business suits had been moved into place after arriving in Luanda, Angola the night before. They crossed the Angolan-Namibian border in a car and caught a train to Luanda. Higgs had sent them to hijack the flight from Luanda to Johannesburg. They planned to land the airplane on a remote airfield near the Angolan-Namibian border.

They had weapons to hijack the plane—plastic guns that looked like parts of a tape player with a gun barrel that looked like a fountain pen—in their briefcases. Their guns were easily assembled and could not be detected by the X-ray scanning equipment in the security system at the airport. The ammunition looked like steel marbles that one of the men carried in his carry-on luggage in a plastic bag full of real marbles, disguising them as a gift for his kids.

They had been ordered to board the plane the US ambassador's daughter was going to take, Flight 283 from Luanda to Johannesburg, leaving from Gate 22 at ten thirty in the morning. The flight was just an hour and a half long, but they planned to commandeer the plane right after it reached its cruising altitude, which was only a few minutes into the flight. Their plan was to land it on a runway in the mountains of Angola near the Namibian border and kidnap Renée and her friends. They were going to use them as leverage to gain concessions from the Mandela-led South African government. They would let the other passengers and the flight crew continue to

Johannesburg after holding them for twenty-four hours. This would give the kidnappers time to meet their comrades and drive across the Namibian border to a remote Inkatha militia training camp in the Drakensberg Mountains of Natal Province, South Africa.

The TWA flight from New York landed on schedule in Luanda. Renée, Denise, Tina and Michelle deplaned. They were exhausted from their long flight but still quite excited. They had never been in Luanda before, and they really wanted to see everything they could before catching the flight to Johannesburg. Their baggage would be transferred to South African Airways Flight 283. The girls walked around the airport taking, in the sights and looking at the people in business suits and traditional dresses.

The sightseeing gave them an opportunity to stretch their legs after being cooped up in an airplane for twenty hours. They were somewhat restricted about where they could walk because they were not going through Angolan customs, but they carried their passports just in case they were stopped.

The posse was laughing and discovering together. The other girls did not notice that four white businessmen were closely watching their every move. Renée felt a twinge of suspicion when two of these men signaled each other while looking at the girls.

Something is not quite right! Maybe they are just admiring four pretty young ladies, she thought, *I shouldn't be so paranoid.* She looked at her friends and laughed to herself. *I think we look pretty whipped.*

They boarded Flight 283 to Johannesburg, and the plane taxied down the runway. The four girls were seated in the middle of the Boeing 767. The airplane was almost full with at least 250 passengers. People were traveling to South Africa to take part in the celebrations of the all-race elections despite the violence and resistance.

"Just another hour and a half till we're there," said Renée.

"And not soon enough for me. Once I get off this airplane, I don't want to see another one take off or land for a month," Tina replied.

Michelle said, "I heard that!"

"You guys know my mom has all kinds of plans for us, including some flights on smaller airplanes to other parts of South Africa," Renée said.

"Yeah, but we're all hoping that won't be for at least a week or so. I sure don't want to fly anymore anytime soon," Denise said.

Tina looked around the plane and turned to her friends. "I wonder if they're going to feed us." She patted her flat tummy. "I'm hungry."

Tina was the tiniest one of the posse, but she ate more than anybody else.

Michelle said, "Tina you're always hungry. They just fed us breakfast before we landed. You should have grabbed something to eat while we were in the airport."

"Yeah, that's true, but I'm still hungry," Tina replied.

The girls continued to talk about their upcoming activities.

The Afrikaner businessmen were seated in different areas of the airplane. The flight flew over the Angolan countryside. After ten minutes, with passengers relaxing and flight attendants making everyone comfortable, one of the men walked to the restroom with his briefcase. The other three followed in one-minute intervals, each carrying a handbag or briefcase.

Inside the restroom, the men assembled the plastic guns. Each nine-millimeter automatic carried a clip with ten bullets. The first man emerged with his briefcase precisely five minutes after he had entered the restroom. The second man came out of the adjacent restroom at the same time; they spoke and exchanged niceties as though strangers and shook hands, surreptitiously exchanging briefcases. The first man's briefcase contained ammunition; the briefcase of the second man contained nothing but newspaper. The first man kept his supply of ammunition.

The other two men came out of their respective restrooms, one behind the other, in time to pass the second man. Inconspicuously, they stopped briefly in the aisle, and the second man handed the other two loaded clips for their plastic guns. No one other than Renée even noticed since it happened so quickly. The two men Renée had seen in the airport were speaking to each other in the aisle. Something was up, but Renée did not see the exchange.

The clips were quickly placed in their pockets, and they returned to their seats. Twenty minutes into the flight, the first man got up from his seat without his briefcase and walked through first class to the cockpit door. The second man moved to the middle of the airplane, the third went to the middle, just twenty feet from the second, and the fourth went to the back. All of the men were in place.

The hijackers wore disguises to be certain they could not be identified. The first hijacker wore a neat moustache and goatee, the second wore a red wig and glasses, the third wore a shaggy blond wig, a fake nose, and horn-rimmed glasses, and the fourth wore a large black moustache, a black wig, and brown contact lenses.

At precisely twenty minutes and thirty seconds into the flight of Flight 283, the first man pulled out his gun. He grabbed the lead flight attendant. Her arms were made immobile, held stiffly by her sides by the powerful arm of the hijacker. He demanded that she open the cockpit door. She did, and he quickly entered and instantly captured the pilots.

"Quietly, hand to me the intercom microphone," the man demanded.

In a hard Afrikaner accent, he announced, "Ladies and gentlemen of Flight 283, I do not want you to become alarmed."

Immediately, the passengers became anxious. One woman began crying. Everyone assumed that they were going to crash.

"Remain calm and remain seated. Your aircraft has been hijacked. No one will be harmed if you just cooperate."

On cue, the other three hijackers pulled their guns and guarded the passengers. Each hijacker reiterated what the first hijacker had said.

"Remain calm, and no one will be hurt," each said with strong Afrikaner accents.

A wave of panic swept through the passengers. The woman who had been crying let out a piercing scream, and a man frantically attempted to get up, not knowing where he was going on a flight that was thirty thousand feet in the air. One of the hijackers quickly and violently knocked the man back into his seat on top of two other passengers. The impact cut him, and blood trickled down his lip. The people who were seated next to him took care of him, wiping his wound with a napkin.

"Remain seated, and remain calm," yelled one of the hijackers, "and we will not harm you!"

Renée and the girls were scared to death but unaware that they were the targets of the hijacking.

The hijacker in the cockpit ordered the captain to maintain radio silence. He shoved a piece of paper into the captain's hand and demanded that he follow the written coordinates for rerouting the plane.

The captain and his copilot shifted the plane toward the east, away from its planned destination. An air traffic controller noticed the sudden change in flight pattern. He desperately tried to contact Flight 283, but it very quickly disappeared from the radar screen. The air traffic controller notified his supervisor about the disappearance.

"It appears that SAA Flight 283 is having trouble," he said. "It's as though it's gone down. I'm afraid that it might have crashed."

They tried to make contact again and again, but still there was no response.

Flight 283 was below radar at an altitude of three thousand feet, flying through valleys at a reduced speed. Only twenty minutes after the airplane had changed its course, a runway appeared in an obscure valley just north of the Namibian border. The pilot was instructed to land the airplane.

"Prepare for landing, ladies and gentlemen. I have just turned on the fasten seatbelt sign. We will be landing shortly," the captain said calmly.

The landing gear was lowered successfully, and the airplane began to descend. The hijackers moved passengers to their seats and sat in the back and front of the plane.

The plane landed roughly and came to a halt at the end of the runway. The first hijacker instructed the flight attendants to open the front door and to keep all passengers in their seats.

The flight attendants quickly unlatched the airplane door and slid it to the side. Immediately, ten Zulu Inkatha militiamen rushed onto the airplane with AK-47 assault rifles. They ran down the aisles and stood guard over the passengers.

Betelema entered the airplane. His villainous eyes scanned each of the passengers. His eyes caught a glimpse of Renée and her friends.

Renée, Tina, Michelle and Denise were terrified. Their eyes were wide and starting to tear. The other girls were looking at Renée with questioning eyes for some answer to what was going on.

Renée looked at Betelema and thought, *Who is this man? What does he want? Why was the plane hijacked? Is there an important person on board?*

With a quick motion of his hand, Betelema signaled four of the militiamen to take Renée and her friends off the airplane. The girls complied with the orders for them to get up. Not a word was spoken.

The militiamen immediately seized the girls. All of them gasped for air, shocked that they were singled out and in fear of what lay ahead. The men took the girls off the plane, and Denise almost passed out.

"Stay calm, you guys. Stay calm," Renée said as they were taken from the plane.

Betelema shook his head, said something to the first hijacker, and left the plane.

The first hijacker watched Betelema leave and turned to the remaining passengers. "Stay in your seats, and you will not be harmed."

Betelema's plan would be carried out. The passengers would remain in their seats, and the crew would feed and care for them under the watchful eyes of the hijackers. Each hijacker would get a four-hour nap while the others kept the passengers and crew under guard. The passengers were allowed to go to the bathrooms two at a time. In twenty-four hours, they would be able to continue their flight to Johannesburg.

CHAPTER 13

The twenty-four-hour delay in the flight would give Betelema and his militiamen enough time to cross the Namibian border and drive across Namibia into the South African province of Natal. They would continue to the mountains of Natal to their hidden campsite deep in Inkatha Zulu-controlled territory.

Once the girls were off the plane, Betelema gave orders to his men in the Zulu language of Natal. "Blindfold and gag the girls, and place them into the second truck." There were four trucks. "The detail I instructed to stay behind and camouflage the landing strip has their orders. Any questions?"

The militiamen replied, "No, sir."

Betelema ordered the rest of his men to the trucks. The militiamen would cover the airfield so well that the pilots of Flight 283 could barely find it. Betelema got into the lead vehicle and signaled the other trucks to follow.

The militiamen left behind would return to their homeland undetected by any South African security.

The four Afrikaner hijackers were to leave the airplane in twenty-two hours and take a vehicle left for them back to headquarters in the Orange Free State.

Renée, Denise, Tina, and Michelle were terrified, uncertain of their fate, and did not know who had abducted them or why. They didn't know where they were or where they were going. They only knew several black African military men led by a big man who was their commander had kidnapped them with the assistance of white Afrikaners. They were confused by that camaraderie.

Renée thought, *Why were we singled out amongst the more than 250 passengers of Flight 283? Did they know that I am the ambassador's daughter? They must have.*

The trucks continued to ramble through the uninhabited country for hours. The girls heard the men talking loudly in their native Zulu language, but they couldn't understand a word.

Renée could hear the muffled sobs of Denise. *What are they planning to do to us?* Renée thought in desperation. Tina and Michelle were silent.

The trucks finally stopped, and the girls heard of a lot of soldiers.

Someone with a strong Afrikaner accent asked, "Did you get them? Was there any resistance? Where are they?"

Betelema gave Higgs the details of the mission and told him all had gone as planned. He spoke in English to Higgs, and the two men were within earshot of the girls.

Higgs looked at the girls in the back of the truck. Satisfied, he returned to where Betelema was standing. The four hijackers were still on the airplane and would be releasing the pilots, crew, and passengers in exactly eight hours and forty-eight minutes. The two unlikely allies spoke for a few more minutes about the details of their plan and parted company. Higgs got into a Hummer and departed to the southwest with his entourage.

Betelema returned to the lead truck of his caravan. They had crossed the Angolan-Namibian border and traveled across Namibia undetected. They were now in Botswana driving toward the mountains near Zimbabwe outside of Kwagen Park. They had to continue rapidly in order to reach their destination within eight hours. Betelema wanted to be safely in their mountain encampment hideout before Flight 283 resumed its flight to Johannesburg.

Betelema and his men were going to use Renée and her friends as bargaining chips. Their capture was the leverage needed in the African Freedom Alliance's effort to have the permanent constitution include their goals for power and autonomous homeland areas in Kwazulu for Zulus and Orange Free State for white ultraconservative Afrikaners.

The South African government air authorities had been notified, but no one knew what had happened to Flight 283. Angolan air authorities had been notified that it had disappeared from the radar screens and were searching the data for any clues about where the flight might have gone down or crashed. It was all a mystery.

CHAPTER 14

Ambassador and Mrs. Davis had been notified that Flight 283 was missing. They were not certain about whether the flight had crashed, was destroyed, or was hijacked. Horace and Beverly were horrified. What could have happened to the flight?

Horace said, "Honey, I know they are just fine. They probably are just having some radar problems or something." He knew deep down that she didn't buy this explanation, but he didn't know what else to say. His forehead was wrinkled with signs of dread.

Streams of tears gently ran down Beverly's face.

Both were extremely distressed about the disappearance of their daughter's flight. Horace was trying his best to stay strong and positive. He had not given up on the safe finding of Renée and her friends.

"Horace, I know you are trying to make me feel better. But I know my instincts, and something's really wrong. I can feel it! Renée's okay; she is not dead. I'd know if one of my own children had died. I'd feel it with my whole being, but I know something is wrong. Terribly wrong!"

Beverly's belief in Renée's safety comforted Horace. However, a chill of horror engulfed him when Beverly was so adamant that something was terribly wrong.

Both of them were keenly aware of all the political strife that encircled the elections. Before, during, and even after the elections, terrorist activities were being carried out all over the country. Bombings and killings happened almost daily. It was not beyond any of the terrorist groups to attack an airline. Beverly was worried about Renée and her friends.

Horace was on the telephone, demanding that the South African government investigate the situation immediately and inform him about what had transpired.

Jon Vanholder left his office and briskly walked to the situation room. He was the director of the Department of Civil Aviation of South Africa. He had been notified about the disappearance of Flight 283 from radar and knew the US ambassador's daughter was on the flight.

Vanholder was a white man in his fifties who wore his reddish-brown hair combed straight back to cover the spot where his hair had thinned. His green eyes were serious and reflected his alertness. He had worked his way up from air traffic controller to his present position with twenty-five years of hard work. He was a neat dresser, organized, and expected his staff to be efficient.

Heidi Semelburg, his chief assistant, briefed him when he arrived. There were about twenty or thirty other aviation technicians in the task force room. Kronen Heist was a navigation specialist, and Helmut Schultz was the liaison between civilian airlines and military air forces.

The room was located on the lower level of the Department of Aviation building. It was built like a bunker with thick concrete and steel walls surrounding it. Military guards were stationed at the entrance. Top-secret clearance was necessary to enter the room. Inside, aviation technicians operated rows of specialized computers. The walls were covered with big screens of electronic maps, radar, tracking devices, high-tech surveillance information, and various grids. There were also high-tech communications telephones and screens that connected other areas to the room.

"Give me an update on the status of the search," Vanholder said after a brief greeting to those directly involved.

"The search aircraft will be airborne in twenty minutes," Heidi replied. "Pilots are in the briefing room as we speak, being given all the information we have on the Flight 283. We have only two hours of daylight left, and the search will end when it starts getting dark. We'll resume at dawn. We're going to be coordinating the search with a search team from Luanda since the last report from the flight's pilots came while they were still in Angola. We're praying that the airplane just lost its communications system somehow. However, the US ambassador's daughter is on that flight, and heaven forbid, this could be a hijacking by one of the dissenting organizations."

Schultz said, "The military is available for aid in the search, if necessary. I have alerted General Ottman of the situation, and his pilots are on standby alert. If this is anything other than an unfortunate accident, a mishap, then I don't believe this is going to be a routine civilian matter. Grave political circumstances may be at hand, which mean serious consequences for whoever may be involved."

Vanholder and his staff urgently turned to the screen to follow and coordinate the search.

CHAPTER 15

The trucks finally came to a stop after hours of rambling through hot, dusty lowlands and then steadily climbing in sweltering humid heat. The girls' blindfolds and gags were still in place. They still had no idea where they were, who their captors were, or why they were kidnapped. They only knew that they were frightened of the unknown captors, hot from the sweltering heat, tired from their long journey, sore from the drive, and hungry because they had not eaten since breakfast.

Renée heard the voices of men in the trucks and many more outside of the trucks. She could smell the cooking of food and hear the activity of a bustling camp. For some reason, she found the voice of the man who was in command familiar. Everyone sounded very excited, yet under control.

Suddenly, soldiers removed the gags and blindfolds.

"Oh, my God. We're in the middle of a jungle," Renée said.

The other girls looked around distressed, shocked, and amazed. Their eyes widened with horror to find themselves in the absolutely unfamiliar surroundings of a mountain jungle militia camp. Renée saw about two hundred soldiers roaming around the camp in camouflaged fatigues. It was a training camp for the Zulu Inkatha Freedom Party militia.

The trucks had been ascending up a mountain for at least an hour. The camp was in a cleared mesa area at the top of a mountain. They could see about ten barracks that housed the soldiers.

A larger structure in the middle of the camp was the headquarters and the living quarters of the commander. On the outside perimeter, two guard towers faced down the mountain toward the road.

Renée thought, *Soldiers are probably on duty in these towers twenty-four hours per day.*

There was a mounted machine gun in each of the towers. Near the headquarters, there was a shower and latrine house. The kitchen and mess hall were next to the headquarters. The camp had been built when the Inkatha Zulus continuously struggled against apartheid and the ANC. The back of the camp was buttressed by dense jungle.

Renée, Tina, Michelle, and Denise looked around the camp and at the men, trying to get their blinking eyes to focus on where they had been taken. They saw only trees and jungle. Not a word was spoken. Their eyes met and communicated their fright.

Two militiamen led the girls to a barrack house with a door that led into a large room with four bunk beds. Next to the room was a bathroom with a small window. The barrack was to be guarded twenty-four hours per day with armed militiamen. Almost immediately after the girls were placed in the barrack, a young soldier brought them food and drinks. Silently, the soldier left the barrack and closed the door.

Even though the girls were terrified, they were also famished. They pounced on the food. They devoured everything set before them. There was chicken, beans, rice, greens, and baked bread. They gulped down the cokes that had been chilled for them along with a large pitcher of cold water. After all they could swallow had disappeared from their plates, the complete silence between them was finally broken.

"What's going on?" Tina asked, trying to catch her breath after their marathon meal. "Renée, who in the hell are these people? Why did they kidnap us?"

"Shhhhhh. They may be listening," Michelle said, glancing around the room. "Where the hell are we?"

"What are they going to do to us?" Denise asked.

Question upon question upon question were directed at Renée. She felt like she was being blamed for their fate. She definitely didn't have the answers to any of their questions. She was in the dark and just as desperate as the others. They were all very scared.

Suddenly, the door opened, startling the girls. Renée abruptly turned her focus to the individuals coming toward them. Silence filled the room again. The girls were holding their breath. The only sound that resonated throughout the room was the footsteps of those entering the barrack.

Betelema walked in with four militiamen. He smiled at the frightened girls and said, "Welcome to South Africa, Renée, Denise, Tina, and Michelle." He nodded toward each of them as he said their names.

The girls looked at each other as though he had revealed a secret that no one could possibly know without reading their minds.

He paused to clear his throat. "We have brought you to this place as our guests in order to persuade the new parliamentary powers here in South Africa to make certain changes to our new constitution."

Betelema began to pace back and forth in front of the table without losing eye contact. "Upon achieving this goal, you will be returned to your father, Ambassador Davis, Renée, with your friends." His menacing glare sent chills through Renée's body. "Until this occurs, you are guests, but your movements in and around our camp will be monitored. Do not attempt to escape from this camp. Not because we will do harm to you but because surrounding us is jungle that is home to many wild animals—lions, leopards, hyenas, snakes—you get the picture." Betelema smiled widely, almost showing all of his teeth, relishing in his successful attempt to frighten the girls even more. "Also, you do not know where you are." His demeanor suddenly changed as though he was a perfect, gentle host. "You will be treated with respect and dignity. My men have been so ordered. If there is anything that you need, just ask. Your guards speak English."

Betelema scrutinized each of the girls with a long admiring stare, said something to his men in the Zulu language, and walked out.

The door opened again almost instantaneously, and the militiamen came into the barrack with the girls' suitcases. They placed them in the middle of the room and turned and left, closing the door behind them.

Renée and her friends were frozen in place and looked at each other in panicked silence.

CHAPTER 16

After twenty-two hours, the passengers of Flight 283 were too exhausted to be hysterical. Quiet breathing had engulfed the aircraft. Passengers were slumped in their seats. They had depleted all their energy in the initial hours of the panic after being hijacked. They perspired profusely from the excruciating heat and humidity of the Angolan sun. At least they thought that was where they were.

Suddenly, the silence was broken. The time had come. The hijacker in the cockpit instructed the pilot to prepare for takeoff. Overhearing this order, the anxious and tired passengers became alert. The four hijackers signaled to each other and exited the aircraft. The flight attendants closed and secured the door and then began to instruct everyone to fasten their seatbelts.

Loud roars resounded from the passengers. They cheered joyfully, relieved that they were finally flying away to their original destination just dehydrated and otherwise unharmed.

The aircraft started up and began to taxi to the end of the jungle landing strip under the watchful eyes of the soldiers left behind to guard it. The plane taxied down the short runway, just gaining enough momentum and speed to lift into the air and soar away from their captives. The hijackers had destroyed all the plane's radio equipment, and transmission could not be made. Once airborne, the airplane turned south and soon disappeared. The four hijackers had already entered their Hummer and headed toward South Africa. There was a nod between the Afrikaner hijackers and the Inkatha militiamen.

The militiamen covered the landing field with brush and foliage to camouflage its location. The landing strip now looked like the surrounding jungle. The militiamen retreated back to their homelands in South Africa. The mission had been completed.

CHAPTER 17

Flight 283 had been in the air for just forty-five minutes when it was spotted by a South African Air Force jet. The search had resumed at first light, and the skies from Luanda to Johannesburg were filled with military and civilian search teams. The pilot of the Air Force jet flew alongside the passenger plane and signaled the pilots to follow him. He radioed the task force headquarters and told them that they were going to guide Flight 283 to a secluded airstrip in the Jan Smit Airport in Johannesburg.

Horace and Beverly Davis, Jon Vanholder and his staff, top political and security brass, relatives of the passengers, and a horde of reporters from all over the world were anxiously awaiting the arrival of Flight 283. Because of the lack of radio communications, people could only speculate about what had transpired.

The airplane landed and rolled to a halt in the middle of the airfield. Emergency vehicles, police, military personnel, and political envoys rushed to the plane as a precaution in order to immediately assist any passengers who had been injured in the ordeal. The passenger door finally opened, and a flight attendant appeared at the door and held back passengers eager to get off while stairs were brought to the aircraft and put in place.

The passengers began to deplane, one at a time. Horace and Beverly were in the front of the crowd that surrounded the plane. Beverly stretched her neck and stood on her tiptoes to get a better look at the passengers and the plane. The last of the passengers finally descended the steps of the aircraft. Beverly did not see any sign of Renée and the other girls.

Beverly looked at Horace in utter disbelief. She hoped that her husband had seen Renée coming out of the plane. Her whole body trembled with the fear that Horace had seen what she had seen—no sign of Renée.

Horace grabbed Beverly and rushed to talk to the general in charge of the search.

Beverly tried to keep her composure. "Where is Renée? I didn't see her come off the plane." Her heart was pounding so hard that she could feel it in her throat.

"Everyone who was on the aircraft has exited the plane. There are no other passengers on board," the general said.

Horace and Beverly were devastated! Where was their daughter? Who had taken her and her friends?

Relatives and friends of the other passengers were excited to have their loved ones returned to them relatively unharmed. Beverly was devastated as she watched the joyful reunions of the passengers and their loved ones. Her baby was missing. It was all too obvious that the hijacking was carried out to kidnap Renée and her friends, but no ransom demands or political demands had been made, and there had not been any communication from any of the many dissenting groups in South Africa.

The South African police and Secret Service and the FBI and US Secret Service interrogated passengers and crew to obtain as much information as possible. Police sketch artists spoke with passengers and crew to get sketches of the four Afrikaner hijackers and the Zulu military commander who took the four girls.

Military planes were sent to search for the jungle airfield in Angola or Namibia, near the border. President Mandela was notified that the US ambassador's daughter had been kidnapped along with her three friends. The task force room changed its purpose and top military personnel were brought in to assist with the logistics of the search and the preparation of a response plan for whenever they were contacted by an individual or organization taking responsibility.

Johannesburg was very busy. The kidnapping of the ambassador's daughter had grave consequences for relations between the new government and the United States. Rapid and decisive action had to be taken by the South African government in cooperation with the United States, but who were the captors—and where were they?

The military and investigative agencies continued their searches and hoped for contact with the perpetrators.

CHAPTER 18

Betelema and Higgs sat down at their rendezvous in the mountains near the border between Transvaal and Natal.

Betelema was proud of the way the plan was working.

Higgs was also cautiously satisfied with the success of the plan, but he had his doubts about Betelema's ability to complete it. He thought, *I hope I can trust him. These Zulus aren't very smart.* He had no choice; they had to finish what they had started.

The two men continued to set aside their hatred for each other and their respective political parties. Each of them had something to gain from cooperating, which was worth more than despising one another. They adamantly believed that a white Afrikaner homeland and a Zulu homeland controlled by the Inkatha Party had to survive this new democratic government controlled by the ANC Party.

A Zulu soldier and Betelema brought in beer, and Higgs rigidly toasted the success of their hijacking and kidnapping operation.

Betelema looked at Higgs, raised his glass, and in Afrikaner, then Zulu, and finally English, made a toast to their success. "To the success of a well-planned and well-executed mission and to the further implementation of our plan."

Higgs raised his glass and also toasted the mission in Zulu, Afrikaner, and English. "To the successful completion of this undertaking and to the sovereign Afrikaner homeland and the sovereign Zulu homeland."

They heartily drank their beer, set down their mugs, and faced each other in all seriousness. They would make their demands under the name the United African Front.

The two men reviewed the demands that each had prepared as conditions for the return of Renée and her friends.

Higgs and his Afrikaner separatist group demanded an Afrikaner homeland. It called for an autonomous and sovereign homeland for the white separatist group, which would be governed entirely by the homeland's elected officials, almost as if it were a country within a country, having very little connection with the black majority government of South Africa.

Betelema and his splinter group of Inkatha Zulu nationalists drafted their demands for another separated regional homeland in traditional Kwazulu, comprised of only Inkatha Zulus and led by King Zwelthuma, also with total autonomy and self rule. These conditions would need to be provided for in the new constitution to be drafted by the newly elected Parliament. Once drafted, the demands would be delivered to the main television station in Johannesburg.

An emissary from the United African Front took a package into the SBSF television station in Johannesburg at seven in the morning, forty-two hours after the hijacking of Flight 283 and twenty hours after its arrival in Johannesburg. The large envelope was delivered to the receptionist at the front desk. It was addressed to the television station manager. *Urgent* was scribbled across the front in bold red letters. Without a word, the courier abruptly turned and left after handing the envelope to the receptionist. The receptionist examined the envelope momentarily and then got up to look for the station manager.

John Rutterman, the station manager, was on the telephone in his office. He signaled for the receptionist to come in when she appeared at the door to his office and gestured with the large envelope.

The receptionist entered the office and handed John the envelope. He excused himself for a moment from his call and examined the outside of the envelope. Satisfied that it was not a bomb or otherwise booby-trapped, he opened it. Inside was a typed communiqué from an organization calling itself the United African Front. It claimed that it was the group that had hijacked Flight 283 and had kidnapped the US ambassador's daughter and her friends. It further stated that it did so in order to ensure that its demands would be implemented. The communiqué continued, stating that the ambassador's daughter and her companions were fine and would remain so if the demands were carried out in the constitution, ratified, and guaranteed. If the Parliament and President Mandela did not carry out these demands, the girls would be executed. The United African Front's communiqué also asserted that if there were any attempts to rescue the girls, they would be executed before the rescuers could reach them.

Rutterman immediately called the government police service to inform them that he had received what appeared to be an authentic demand communiqué. The police immediately dispatched a security agent to retrieve the demands.

Jon Vanholder received the demands and read them. He then handed them to Heidi Semelburg. After she had read the communiqué, Jon said, "Call Horace Davis." Once Ambassador Davis was on the telephone, Jon picked it up.

"Ambassador Davis, this is Jon Vanholder from the South African task force. I have received a communiqué from a group calling itself the United African Front, making demands for separate homelands in new South Africa. They also state that they are the group responsible for hijacking SAA Flight 283 and kidnapping your daughter and her friends. They assured us in this communiqué that your daughter and her friends are safe and being treated well, but they warn that we must carry out their demands and if a rescue is attempted, your daughter and her friends will be executed."

Jon assured the ambassador that all resources available to the South African government would be utilized—and President Mandela was being kept informed as well. He had been authorized by the president to use whatever means necessary with cooperation from the US government to rescue Horace's daughter and her friends unharmed.

"I will keep you informed about the progress of the task force, Mr. Ambassador."

"Thank you for your efforts, Mr. Vanholder. I will be awaiting your next call."

Horace hung up the telephone and looked into the space outside the window of his office, tears welling up in his eyes. He felt relief that the perpetrators had made a demand and that his daughter and her friends were all right. This feeling was followed by an intense anger welling up inside of him. He leaped from his chair, knocked over the books on his desk, and yelled, "Where in the hell do you have my daughter?"

John Douglas and Horace's secretary ran into his office to see what had happened. They calmed him down.

Horace said, "I've got to call my wife."

The secretary called Beverly, and Horace said, "Beverly a television station in Johannesburg received a demand letter this morning about Renée and her friends." He paused just for a second to gather himself.

Beverly had to sit down; she felt very faint.

Horace continued, "It said that Renée and the girls are okay."

Beverly let out a little yelp of relief and asked for more detail.

Horace told her what was in the demand letter and shared his conversation with Jon Vanholder.

CHAPTER 19

All the intelligence agencies were on high alert. Meetings were being held, and there was constant communication between the various agencies and their counterparts in South Africa.

Horace called Washington immediately after updating and consoling Beverly. He brought his boss, the secretary of state, up to date. The secretary of state had already met with the Secret Service director, the FBI director, CIA chief, national security advisor, and the chairman of the Joint Chiefs of Staff to discuss the events of the past forty-eight hours. They had begun mapping out a plan to determine how to react to this crisis in international relations.

Ambassador Davis demanded the rescue of his daughter and her friends. The Secretary of State told the ambassador about the activity that was underway in Washington. The State Department was gathering as much intelligence as possible before deciding on a response. Secretary of State Walter Christian did not want to act unilaterally; he wanted input from all the other departments and agencies before reporting to the president. He also wanted to talk to his South African counterpart to try to determine who these people could possibly be.

Information was also coming in about the location of the airfield. The directional coordinates and time between when Flight 283 left the hidden airfield and when it was intercepted by the military airplane allowed the technical people in the search and rescue task force to narrow the search area down to a fifty square miles just north of the Angolan-Namibian border. With this information, Secretary Christian felt he was now ready to meet with the president and his chief White House security advisory council to discuss a rescue plan. Secretary Christian was a small man with graying brown hair. He was in his early sixties and had been involved in politics since his college days at Colgate University. He always gathered all the facts before making any presentations to the president, his advisory staff, Congress, or the media.

Before entering the Oval Office, Christian straightened his tie.

President Benson and Chief of Staff Thomas O'Leary were waiting when the president's secretary announced him.

Christian entered the Oval Office and greeted the president and O'Leary warmly.

President Benson was the opposite of Secretary Christian. The president was six feet four and weighed 225 pounds. He was in his late fifties. He had been a high school football lineman and an avid tennis player. He still played a good game of tennis and prided himself on being in good shape. He had a great stock of hair, and some said he touched it up because there was not a hint of gray in his sandy blond hair. Mark Benson had been in politics a long time. He had been elected to Congress at twenty-nine and served three terms before being elected to the US Senate where he became one of the young lions. He came into the national spotlight as an environmental advocate and became a very popular moderate democrat from Minnesota. He had rugged good looks and appealed to the female voters. His politics were domestically oriented, but he did pretty well with foreign politics with a global approach to trade, peacekeeping, and environmental policy. He had been a strong supporter of the abolition of apartheid in South Africa and had instituted sanctions against that government until its transition to a democracy. President Mandela considered President Benson one of his strongest allies.

Thomas O'Leary was around the same age as the president. In fact, they had gone to high school together and played on the same football team. O'Leary had been in Congress with the president but had served only two terms, losing his bid for a third. He joined a Washington law firm after his defeat and kept his hand in politics. When Benson decided to run for the presidency, he asked his old friend, teammate, and tennis partner to run his campaign. After the president was elected, Benson asked him to stay on as his White House chief of staff.

Christian moved right to the purpose of the meeting. The president had been notified about the hijacking and kidnapping. He was also aware of the demands made by the group responsible. After his briefing, Christian said, "A rescue must be made and must be swift and successful so as to not encourage this or any other group to feel that this is a valid method of making the South African or any other government acquiesce to their demands. Governments around the world cannot allow terrorist groups to bully them into legislating their demands. South Africa is finally attempting to make the transition from apartheid to democracy and cannot have that process held hostage."

President Benson nodded. "Walter, I give you full authority to carry out a rescue mission with the sanction of the South African government. I want to be kept fully informed about the progress of this effort. Please report to Thomas. He will assist you in any way needed to expedite the rescue effort."

With that said, the men stood and shook hands.

"I will stay in touch and keep you informed as we formulate the rescue plan and then implement it. Good day, Mr. President... Mr. O'Leary." Christian turned and left the Oval Office.

Secretary Christian convened his rescue task force. He had called on the chairman of the Joint Chiefs of Staff, General Genoa Sheppard, the top military officer in the United States, his crisis task force head, Major General Rocky Moreno, and their attachés. The plan would be devised in the next twenty-four hours, and they were to meet again to discuss this plan and the logistics of its implementation.

Twenty-four hours later, the crisis task force met again.

Major General Moreno said, "The area near the location believed to be where Flight 283 was landed by the hijackers is in an almost totally black African population. A white American rescue team would be spotted and reported within an hour of being dropped into the area to search for the kidnapped victims. Therefore, an African American and a black South African rescue team must be used in this operation. They must look like any safari or tourist group traveling in the area in order for their mission to go undetected. If this task force and the South African task force agree, then I will put together the right people for the mission guided by South African military personnel. Reconnaissance aircraft have been taking photographs of the areas where the South African task force suspected the girls may be held. The last photographs taken from an altitude of forty-five thousand feet showed a camp in very rough jungle terrain with only one mountain road leading to it. The photographs also showed two girls in civilian clothes walking inside the camp. One of the girls' faces could be seen, and she was identified as Denise Ortega, one of the girls who was kidnapped with the ambassador's daughter. The camp has been pinpointed, and Angolan troops have found the jungle airfield. It was an old airfield used by Angolan rebels and ANC militia, but it was abandoned a few years ago."

Major General Moreno then paused to field questions or comments. All of the participants were taking notes and listening intently. No questions or comments were presented, so he continued,

"We now know where the camp is and who the captors are generally but not specifically. Our plan cannot be perfected until we gather more information, and then a precise strategy must be devised. The right personnel must be selected, trained, and prepared for the rescue operation."

After General Moreno completed his presentation, he asked his colleagues on the Crisis Task Force if they had any questions.

"How much time do you think will be necessary to be ready to go forward with the rescue?" Secretary Christian asked.

"We must be ready to go in no more than five days. It is going to take that much time to select the right personnel, train them, duplicate models of the jungle camp where the girls are being held, and coordinate the rescue with the South African task force. With the approval of this task force, we will move forward and implement our plan with deliberate speed. We want to get those captives out of there as quickly as possible. According to the demand letter, the girls are being treated well. And our surveillance team that took pictures of the two girls did not detect any injuries to them. We do not want to put them in harm's way by carrying out this rescue."

With that said, the task force voted to go ahead with the plan. General Moreno would report back to the crisis task force in five days.

CHAPTER 20

Major General Moreno went to Fort Bragg to brief Colonel Tate about the mission and to enlist his help in identifying the right personnel for the rescue team. Tate had served under General Moreno in Vietnam and other special assignments throughout their careers. There was a strong friendship and mutual admiration between the two.

Together they would assemble the rescue team and train them in a hurry. The two military men sat down in a briefing room after fond greetings and began discussing the plan.

Colonel Marvin Tate was a career military man. He had gone to West Point and graduated with honors. He had done two tours of duty in Vietnam and sustained a leg wound that completely healed. He had been awarded the Purple Heart, the Medal of Valor, and the Army Cross.

Marvin was a black man in his early forties. Having been in the jungles of Vietnam, he understood jungle operations. He was a "full-bird" colonel, the highest ranking for a colonel in the US Army, and head of training for Army Special Forces at Fort Bragg, North Carolina. He had spent time in Nicaragua and El Salvador to secretly train rebel soldiers for the CIA.

Marvin's career had bogged down a little. He felt it was time he was moved into the Pentagon as the assistant to the commander of Special Forces for the army. He had the most distinguished record in the Special Forces, and he had been passed over twice for this promotion. He knew that he was more qualified than the two officers selected before him, but they were more politically connected. Major General Rocky Moreno was in a position to help him move up. Marvin knew this was a very important mission, probably the one that would propel his career to that job in the Pentagon.

Marvin was not a big man. He was five feet ten, lean, and hard at 175 pounds. He was a fourth-degree black belt in karate, the master of several martial arts disciplines, and could kill or maim a man with a single blow to the right spot. Hand-to-hand combat was his specialty.

The team of rescuers was going to be made up of six soldiers, and since their cover was going to be a family on safari, female soldiers were going to be an integral part of the team. The team would have to act swiftly and silently to get the girls out without jeopardizing their lives. Explosives were going to be used for diversions and weapons.

"We need an expert who can shoot any type of weapon necessary for the rescue. This person must be able to assemble weapons carried in boxes or suitcases," General Moreno said. "This soldier must be an expert marksman, a sniper who can shoot at long distances and has experience in using night-vision equipment."

Marvin nodded and thought for a minute. "I have just the man for this mission, Sergeant Edward R. Jackson. Eddie Jackson is a career soldier. He's been enlisted for eight years, looks like a new recruit, but he's twenty-six. He's the top marksman on the base—he eats and sleeps weapons. He can take most weapons apart and put them back together, perfectly, with his eyes closed. Yeah, he's our man."

After Eddie Jackson graduated from Central High School in St. Joseph, Missouri, he joined the army because he wanted to get out of that one-horse town and see the world. His father had been in the army during the Korean War and had been to Korea, Japan, China, Hawaii, and all over the United States. Eddie was the youngest of seven children, and he hadn't been anywhere outside of Kansas and

Missouri. As soon as he finished high school, he had to see the world. He joined the army and was sent to Fort Benning, Georgia, for his basic training. His father and uncles were hunters, and Eddie had grown up around guns. He had been shooting rifles, shotguns, and handguns since he was eight. He demonstrated an outstanding ability with weapons and qualified as a top marksman. Since enlisting, he had earned a reputation as a marksman and a flamboyant, fun-loving soldier. He enjoyed a good time and the ladies. However, he didn't drink because he didn't want anything to interfere with his steady hand. He was always under control, a good soldier.

"Okay Marvin," General Moreno said. "Put him on the team."

"Sure thing, Rocky," Marvin replied.

"I think we need a good explosives expert. We need one who can move silently and quickly to put explosives into place whenever necessary. One who knows what different explosives can do and how to use them. Who do you suggest, Marvin?"

Marvin thought for a few minutes and then replied, "Harry Washington is the demolitions expert that I'm going to choose. He's a corporal in the demolition division of the Special Forces. He has been in the army for four years and loves blowing things up. He said that he fell in love with watching fireworks when he was a kid. He became a helper with the fireworks at the park in his neighborhood where he was a teenager."

Harry Washington was twenty-two, a bit wild and cool, but he fit into the mission well because he appeared to be so young that he would not alert anyone to the fact that he was an experienced soldier. In this rescue mission, he would appear more like a kid on vacation with his father, mother, sister, brothers, and guides.

Harry had joined the army after high school to get into demolitions. His father, brother, and girlfriend in Springfield, Illinois, wanted him to go to college. He was a pretty good athlete and a smart student. He had won an academic and athletic scholarship to a small college in Illinois and probably could have made the basketball team as a starting guard, but that wasn't for him at the time. He did plan to attend college and had even finished several courses at a junior college in Fayetteville, North Carolina, but the major portion of his college education was on hold until he got this explosives thing out from under his skin.

Colonel Tate said, "I know just the right soldier for the role of sister on this rescue mission, Rocky. I don't even have to think about this one because she came to mind as soon as we devised this rescue plan. Captain Donna Rhodes is a cross-country skier and expert marksman, or marksperson, I believe is correct when referring to female competitions. She had a spot on the 1992 Winter Olympic Team in the ski and shoot competition. I don't remember whether she won a medal or not, but she's one of the best in the world in this event. They had to cross-country ski to a target carrying an M-16 rifle, stop at a target, take their best shot, and then ski to the next target, and repeat it until they'd finished the course. I believe they were judged by the accuracy of the shooting and the time it took them to complete the course. She's in great shape. She also served in Operation Desert Storm, as did the other soldiers I recommended, and will recommend."

Rocky listened and nodded in approval.

Colonel Tate supplied a personnel file to him for each of the soldiers chosen for the mission, and he followed along as Marvin introduced his team.

Donna Rhodes was an outstanding army officer, and she had been a very intelligent and remarkable college student. Donna attended Hampton University in Virginia and graduated cum laude from the business school. She had also completed four years of ROTC training and entered the army to do her four-year stint as a first lieutenant.

Captain Rhodes had a black belt in karate and tae kwon do, and she was quite capable in hand-to-hand combat with any man. She was a beautiful woman in her early twenties with olive skin and shoulder-length dark hair. She had a pleasant smile and an easygoing personality. Her future plans were to return to Los Angeles, go to law school, and open a family law practice to help abused women and children. For now, she was a soldier, and as usual, she wanted to be the best one in her division. She was ready for combat and would fit the team and its assignment perfectly. To anyone watching the Americans on the safari, Donna would appear to be the sister and daughter in the family.

The next member of the team had to be an older woman. Major Bonita Taylor, a career officer, was the soldier of choice.

Marvin said, "Major Taylor will round out the team. She's the mother figure we need and an excellent soldier. I have already spoken to her, and she is anxious to go on this rescue mission. Rocky you know Major Taylor could have turned this thing down because she's up for a promotion and reassignment to Fort McHenry in Washington. She's just waiting for the paperwork, but she wants to be part of this and help rescue these girls. We really need her, and I am grateful that she agreed to be part of our team."

Major Taylor had been in the army since she graduated from college eighteen years earlier. One of the first female soldiers to train with a combat unit, she looked soft and sweet. She was a no-nonsense soldier, and she had become a combat training officer. She had made many parachute jumps and had combat experience in Grenada, Panama, and Operation Desert Storm. Major Taylor was also an archery expert. She had competed in contests since she was in high school and could kill a fly on the side of the barrack at twenty feet before it could fly away. Her archery skill was an additional asset to the mission. They would be able to disarm the guards from long distance with a silent weapon.

Major Taylor was an attractive woman in her late thirties. She had short black hair and velvety brown skin. She was five feet seven and 130 pounds. Bonita had gotten married right after Operation Desert Storm. Her husband, Lieutenant Colonel Robert Thompson, was an artillery commander. They had agreed to not change her last name for the army, but privately, she did business with a hyphenated Taylor-Thompson last name. Her marriage had changed the direction of her career somewhat because she had decided to apply for a promotion and assignment that would keep her out of combat and get her into administration.

Robert Thompson was a few years older than Bonita. Robert was on the army political fast track and would be transferred to the Pentagon shortly after Bonita moved to Fort McHenry.

Bonita wanted this last assignment to rescue the ambassador's daughter. She was very astute politically, and the transition of South Africa from apartheid to democracy, especially with the election of President Mandela, was important to her, as it was to many African Americans. She wanted the process to succeed and did not want anything to affect the support of the US government. She wanted to be a part of the rescue team, and the team needed her.

"The last soldier needed for this mission is a plain good old combat soldier to help fight, if necessary, just in case we are engaged in a scrimmage with the militia holding the girls captive," said Tate. "If the plan has to deviate, and a battle ensues, a good combat soldier is a must. Corporal Tarik Booker is the combat soldier I want on this team. Tarik is a hardcore street kid from South Central Los Angeles. He joined the army after finishing high school to get away from the street violence, drugs, and other situations. Most of the kids he grew up with had gone to jail for a while or were in jail, in a gang, or doing or selling drugs. He didn't want to stay in that environment and joined the army to keep off the streets."

Tarik Booker had played football at Jordan High School, done some boxing at the YMCA on Vermont and Century Boulevards, worked part-time jobs when he could find them, and generally tried to keep away from trouble and the cops. He was a good defensive end in high school, and a lot of colleges were looking at him. Yet, he decided he would go to the army to get the GI Bill scholarship money before going to college. Tarik was six-four and weighed 240 pounds. He was only twenty years old, but he fought like a street fighter. He loved weapons and could use any of them well, and he could easily carry the big machine guns. Colonel Tate had trained him personally. He was definitely ready for the mission.

The plan was to silently approach the campsite where the girls were being held and disable or eliminate the perimeter guards, whichever was necessary. Then they would locate the barracks where the girls were being held, get them out, and retreat to their pickup point to get out. The rescue was to take place at night or in the early morning to ensure that the majority of the militiamen were asleep and the girls were all in the same barracks at the same time. If the planned rescue went off without a hitch, they would be in and out of there in ten minutes, once they reached the camp. Marvin knew from experience that almost no mission goes through without something going wrong, and he prepared contingency plans just in case.

The reconnaissance flight pictures had allowed the army engineers at Fort Bragg to build a camp that duplicated the campsite where the kidnapped girls were being held. The rescue team would have the model camp to prepare for and rehearse the rescue mission.

The rescue team practiced the rescue again and again and again. They went through simulated training sessions in the model camp. There were briefings and question-and-answer sessions with all the planners and then more practice. They had just four days to prepare for the rescue, and the preparations and briefings were intense.

CHAPTER 21

For four days, the girls were guarded very closely. They were only allowed to walk around a restricted area of the camp. Renée and the girls studied the way the camp was structured. The camp was set up in a circle with the command building in the middle, like a hub and a wheel. Two twenty-foot guard towers were in front of the circle. The back of the camp was buttressed by very dense jungle with no road access. Soldiers with mounted machine guns manned the towers twenty-four hours per day.

Each time the girls walked around the camp, they made mental notes of where the buildings were located in relation to each other. They also noted how each building was being used.

The headquarters building had an antenna mounted on it, and it probably had a radio transmitter inside. Betelema's quarters were in the back of the building. Another building near the headquarters was the mess hall. Soldiers would eat in shifts, always leaving some personnel on duty to guard the camp. The building next to the kitchen and mess hall was a storage building. The girls had seen ammunition, vehicle replacement parts, furniture, and other things being taken in and out of the building. The other buildings appeared to be soldiers' barracks, and the girls' small quarters were situated about forty feet from the headquarters. Renée and her friends whispered to each other about the layout of the camp so that the guards could not hear them. Renée wanted to make sure that everyone was familiar with the camp in case they had an opportunity to escape.

The girls were allowed to wash their clothes at an outdoor wash station that was next to a latrine for the soldiers. They also had a clothesline hung between the latrine and a post in the middle of the camp. They had plenty of clothes, and they only washed towels and washcloths. If they needed to wash underwear, they would hang it in the bathroom of their small barrack. They took showers in an outside shower that the soldiers set up for them. It was next to the wash station and was made private with a canvas that was placed about ten feet high all around the shower.

When Michelle was showering, she looked up and saw a soldier in a tree high above the shower looking at her. She screamed and covered herself with a towel. Betelema ran out of the headquarters building, saw what was happening, grabbed a rifle from one of his soldiers, and shot the peeping Tom. The soldier was only wounded in the arm and survived the fall.

Betelema said, "I made it clear that these girls will be treated with respect. We are soldiers, not heathens. Take care of that soldier's wound and then throw him in the brig for a couple of days." Betelema meant for his orders to be carried out.

The girls had privacy from then on. Renée, Michelle, Tina, and Denise talked to each other in hushed voices so they could not be overheard.

"We've got to come up with a plan to get out of this camp, but first we've got to find out where we are," Renée said.

Tina nodded and said, "I know! We've got to figure out some way to get into that headquarters building to see if there's a map or something that will give us our location. Then we may be able to plan an escape. I believe it's our only hope because I don't think anybody knows where they've taken us."

Denise said, "If they are trying to locate us and rescue us, maybe we should stay put so that if they come for us, we will be here."

Everyone looked at Michelle. She said, "I think we should wait a few more days to see if anyone is going to rescue us. You heard Commander Betelema say there are lions, leopards, snakes, and all kinds of wild animals out there in that jungle. Even if we got out of here, there's no telling what we may run into."

They all looked at each other and nodded.

Renée said, "Okay, you guys. Let's do this. We can plan and work for an escape while we're waiting to be rescued. If a rescue doesn't come in the next few days, we need to plan a way to get out of here. You know these people do not play around. They may seem to care about our comfort now, but I am sure they are planning to kill us if they don't get what they want."

Panic spread through the girls' minds. Somehow, they had to plan to save themselves.

Renée said, "It's going to take a few days to come up with a plan, so we can wait for a while for someone to rescue us."

They all agreed to work on their plan and wait a few more days for a rescue. The girls knew they had to get into the headquarters building in order to find a map, get to a radio, or get some information that could pinpoint their location. They had to come up with a plan to commandeer a vehicle to get out of the jungle camp and down the mountain to a nearby village or town. They had seen the soldiers bringing in prostitutes to the camp on Saturday night. The girls' plan called for the creation of a diversion so that the soldiers who guarded them would not miss one of them. They had to work it out and determine which one of them would attempt to get across the open area of the camp to the headquarters without being detected.

The girls decided that the guards could be distracted by sexy lingerie. They would walk around in full view of the guards in their sexiest panties and bras while one of them went out to shower. They would not feel comfortable walking around undressed like that but desperate situations call for desperate measures. This would give the chosen one of them about twenty minutes to sneak into the headquarters and look around quietly, while not waking up Betelema. It was a good plan, but which one of them was going to have to do it? The girls decided that Renée was the best person to carry it out.

The girls knew that Renée had some experience with radios and radio transmission after operating a ham radio for years so that she could talk to her father wherever he was and to friends she had around the world.

Tina said, "Renée could use the radio in the headquarters office to dial her father's frequency and just leave the transmission open. Our location might be traced before anyone realizes that the radio was on."

Michelle said, "This may work."

Renée replied, "I'll see, you guys. I don't want to risk waking Betelema up."

They looked at each other with fear in their eyes and nodded. They had to try.

On the Saturday nights, the soldiers drank pretty heavily. Even those on duty snuck a few drinks and would not be as alert as usual. The girls decided to wait until the next Saturday, just four more days, to implement the plan.

Renée had to get into that headquarters building.

CHAPTER 22

Jon Vanholder and Major General Moreno stayed in constant communication to be certain they understood and coordinated the rescue plan. They decided that the rescue team would be guided into the mountainous jungles of Natal Province, South Africa, by an elite pair of South African Army Special Forces soldiers, Desmond Moussa and Sofia Tutu. Both had been fighters in the ANC guerrilla forces at one time and had been brought into the South African Army Special Forces shortly before the elections. They were very familiar with the jungles of the Natal Province and knew of the camp where the girls were being held. They were both Zulu and spoke English as well as the dialects of the Zulu and Xhosa tribes spoken in Natal Province.

The US rescue team, code named the Fantastic Six, would meet the South African Army Special Forces guides at an air force base near Durban in Natal Province. After a one-day briefing, they would use a safari vehicle to drive to the Landau Tourist Village Hotel in the Natal homeland area.

The Fantastic Six would be dressed in civilian clothing, looking very much the part of an African American family on a safari vacation with hired South African tour guides. They would check into the resort hotel and then launch their rescue operation from there. They would have camera equipment to take photographs of the wild animals and the scenery in the area. They would act like any other family on a photographic safari to avoid any suspicion or speculation about the real mission. They would try to move toward the mountain jungle where the camp was located without arousing anyone's curiosity.

The plan had further logistical details that had to be worked out, such as where to hide the weapons, the sophisticated reconnaissance equipment, and the communications equipment.

The group was preparing, working, and studying eighteen hours per day. After four days, they would fly to the airbase in South Africa. They would have one day of travel, one day of acclimating to the change in climate and time, and more briefings. After that, they would launch the rescue operation.

Major General Moreno kept General Sheppard apprised of the progress of the rescue operation. He, in turn, informed Secretary of State Christian. Secretary Christian informed the Chief of the White House Staff, Mr. O'Leary, who briefed the president.

Jon Vanholder informed his superiors, including President Mandela. Secretary Christian and Jon Vanholder briefed Ambassador Davis. They assured Ambassador Davis that they were progressing with deliberate speed and that Renée and her friends were unharmed based on the reconnaissance photographs they were continuously taking from forty-five thousand feet above the camp, undetected by their captors. These photographs were scanned and forwarded to Ambassador Davis's office.

CHAPTER 23

On Sunday morning at a quarter to three, Tina opened the door as if to get more air because it was an unusually hot night. She was dressed in black lace bikini panties, a deep-cut bra, and a black lace mini lingerie robe. Renée also came to the door in white silk bikini panties and bra with a short silk robe opened in front to reveal some cleavage.

The guards looked at both girls and began to smile at each other. They looked at the voluptuous Tina and Renée's long velvety brown legs and felt like it was Christmas. Denise and Michelle were also scantily dressed in bikini panties and bras. The partying had subsided, and their guards were nodding a bit. The girls were inside their barrack, waiting for the right moment to commence with their plan

Renée, Tina, Michelle, and Denise were ready to put their plan into action. They decided to start at three o'clock, believing that most of the soldiers would be drunk or asleep by then. Two days earlier, the door of the headquarters building had been left open, and Denise seized the moment to walk onto the porch to ask a soldier for more detergent. Her eyes searched the interior of the structure while he went inside to see if he could comply with the girls' request. Denise outlined the inside of the headquarters for Renée.

Nighttime came, and the soldiers began to party as they had done the previous Saturday night. Prostitutes were brought into the camp in the same trucks that brought Renée and her friends. They were patiently waiting to take action. The soldiers were loud and rowdy, partying and enjoying Saturday night. The partying continued for several hours into Sunday morning. The camp began to quiet down and by 3:00 AM was almost still.

Renée was shaking with fear and anxiety. "If Betelema wakes up and catches me… here I go. Wish me luck."

Renée began speaking to the other girls so that the guards could overhear her. "I can't believe how hot it is tonight. I've been perspiring profusely all day, and I've got to get some relief tonight. I'm going to take a long, cold shower to cool off. This heat is stifling."

"Hurry up because that sounds so good that I'm going to take one too," Tina replied.

The other girls agreed. Renée grabbed a towel and walked past the guards to the outdoor shower. Renée looked back as she walked to the shower. The guards were watching her walk and laughing to each other. They turned around and looked through the door at the other girls who were pretending to play cards at a small table.

The shower was only forty-five feet away. Renée entered the covered area of the shower and turned it on. It was 3:05 a.m. The camp was asleep or otherwise occupied. Renée peeked from behind the cover of the shower at the guard towers and other guard posts. No one was really alert. The guards were talking or sneaking drinks. Renée looked across to the headquarters. She had memorized its layout and only needed ten minutes to find a map or other information so they could figure out where they were and plan an escape.

Renée took a deep breath. *We have to try to escape, but we don't want to get caught. No telling what Betelema would do to us if I get caught.*

The night was overcast and muggy. It was not as bright as it usually was, making it a perfect night. Renée removed her white robe and opened her towel where she had hidden a black sweater and black tights. She put them on quickly and made her way across to the headquarters with catlike moves. She was a fast and graceful runner.

Once on the porch, she checked the guard station again. *So far, so good.* She didn't believe anyone had seen her. She crouched down, moved to the front window, and looked inside. There was a small desk lamp on in the office. No one was inside the office, and the door to Betelema's bedroom was closed. No light came from under his bedroom door.

If I stay low, no one will see me.

She moved quickly and quietly to the door and opened it very slowly. It squeaked slightly. She was frightened, and her heart was pounding so loudly in her ears that it sounded like it had amplifiers. She moved slowly into the room, watching Betelema's bedroom door to see if any light would come on, but none did. Renée moved from desk to desk, staying low and looking at what was on them. Luckily everything was written in English.

She looked at several letters and documents, but nothing gave her a clue about where they were. Finally, she found a map that had an area circled. The circle area said Camp Lunbunda, which was located in Botswana. Maps were on the walls, but she didn't want to stand up to read them. She looked at the clock on a desk; it had been seven minutes since she left the barracks. There was one more shelf with some papers across the room.

I'll go over to that shelf, look at those papers, and get the hell out of here. Renée crouched down once again and moved to the shelf. It was higher than the others, and she had to stand up to reach. She got the papers down, careful not to upend any of the books. One of the papers showed an outline of the airfield where their plane had been forced to land and the route to the camp from the airfield. It also showed that the region where they were being held was in Botswana; Chobekina was down about twenty miles in the lowlands.

She was so excited by her find that she knocked over a book while putting the other papers back. Immediately, a light went on in Betelema's bedroom. Renée scrambled across the room and hid in the well of the desk near to the door. Renée was so scared that she thought her beating heart was going to burst.

Betelema came out in army green boxers and a T-shirt and held a .45 automatic weapon. He looked around the headquarters office. He went to the door and looked out. He could see the girls barrack; the light was on, and the guards were outside. He turned to go back inside, and a small monkey that had been sleeping, one of the pets around the camp, ran out the door. Betelema smiled, took a last look around, went back to his bedroom, closed the door, and turned off the light.

Renée quickly ran to the shower after checking to be sure she would not be seen. She immediately took off her clothes and jumped into the shower. She got wet, toweled off, and put on panties, a bra, and a white robe. She placed her black sweater and tights back into the towel and left the shower. She walked past the guards, with her hair dripping wet, into the barrack, and closed the door. Twelve and a half minutes had passed.

The other girls were so frightened and excited that they were about to faint when Renée had not returned after ten minutes. When she did get back, they were ready to pounce on her to get the details.

"Where have you been? We've all been freaking out," Tina said.

Renée tried to calm herself down. Tears were rolling down her cheeks, and she needed a few moments to get a hold of herself. Renée whispered, "I'm okay. Shh. I did find some things that are going to help us put together a plan."

Denise asked, "What happened? What did you find out about where we are? And how far are we from the nearest town?"

Relieved and exhausted, Renée went over what happened. All of them were excitedly optimistic to have the information they needed to plan their escape.

Tina put on a robe, took a towel, and headed for the shower. She said, "I'll be back in a few."

CHAPTER 24

The Fantastic Six rescue team arrived at an air force base near Durban, South Africa, at six in the morning after an eighteen-hour flight from Fort Bragg, North Carolina. They had been briefed and brought up to date with the latest intelligence. They had trained intensely and were ready for the operation.

It had been six days since the kidnapping. The pirate radio stations near Pretoria and throughout the country were still threatening civil war to establish a white homeland, the Volkstaat. The Volksfront was rapidly losing followers at the extreme right, and any leverage they could muster was important to their very existence.

The rival black factions were still murdering each other at an alarming rate, whether for political reasons or just plain old revenge. The losing factions needed something to boost their political positions. They were still adamant about some kind of autonomy in Zululand and the black homelands.

The news of the kidnapping had been on the front pages in all the newspapers throughout South Africa and the world. Television stations were showing pictures of Renée, Michelle, Tina, and Denise. Editorials were being written about the motivation for the kidnapping and whether the so-called United African Front could succeed in influencing the writing of the permanent constitution in their favor or if it was a last-ditch effort of desperate men.

At seven in the evening, the rescue team had a meeting at the air force base. The soldiers milled around and talked among themselves for a few minutes.

Rocky Moreno and Jon Vanholder entered the room with a South African Air Force general who was the base commander.

"Will you all take your seats?" the base commander said. He waited for a few seconds while the soldiers complied with this request. "I am General Bough Ottman, base commander. Welcome to South Africa. To my right are the two gentlemen who will give you your final orders before embarking on your mission. I wish you Godspeed and good luck in carrying it out. First the American officer head of this rescue mission, Major General Rocky Moreno."

General Moreno stood where he had been seated at the head table facing the soldiers.

General Ottman continued, "Mr. Jon Vanholder, head of the South African task force coordinating the operation to rescue the kidnapped hostages."

Jon Vanholder stood next to his chair at the head of the table.

General Ottman said, "I now turn this briefing over to these gentlemen, and once again soldiers, good luck on this mission. I pray that each of you returns safely." With that, he walked to the head of the table and sat down.

General Moreno said, "Thank you, General Ottman." He turned to acknowledge the general, and then he focused his attention on the soldiers. "Tomorrow at four hundred hours, you will fly to Mauni, Botswana, where an all-terrain vehicle will be waiting for you. This will be your operation vehicle. It will appear to be just another safari vehicle, but it is equipped with the weaponry that you trained with at Fort Bragg. As you were trained and briefed in the States, you will appear to be a family on a photographic safari accompanied by your South African guides. You will arrive at the safari camp in the morning, and from there, you will launch the rescue operation. The team will arrive at the base of the mountain area where the girls are being held. Under the cloak of darkness, you will ascend the mountain to the military camp. The team will enter the camp undetected. After securing the perimeter, swiftly locate the girls, bring them out, and retreat the twenty miles to the rendezvous point where you and the girls will be picked up by South African military helicopters." General Moreno paused to see if any of the soldiers had a question. "Mr. Vanholder will give you some insight about the South African role in this operation."

Vanholder stood next to his chair the entire time that General Moreno made his brief presentation. The rescue team had already been briefed repeatedly. Vanholder decided to also use brevity so that the rescuers could get some sleep. "For the Americans, I welcome you to South Africa." There was practically no hint of an accent in his English. "I know that you have been thoroughly briefed regarding our joint intelligence gathering, so unless there are specific questions, I will not go over that again."

The soldiers who had been listening intently nodded.

Vanholder continued, "I would like to take this opportunity to introduce to the American team your two very capable South African military guides who will take you to the camp in the mountainous jungles in Natal Province where your target subjects are being held captive, Special Forces Sergeants Sofia Tutu and Desmond Moussa." The two South African soldiers immediately stood up to attention next to their chairs.

Vanholder continued, "The all-terrain vehicle will be driven by Sergeant Moussa, and Sergeant Tutu will act as your guide. You have all been given written material describing the background and responsibility of each soldier involved in this rescue and will have ample time to get to know each other during the safari portion of this operation. If there are questions, please address them now." He hesitated, but there were no questions. "Well then, unless General Moreno has anything to add, we will bring this briefing to a close. You have your maps and weapons. Be on the pad ready to depart at 0400 hours. Ladies and gentleman, good luck and our prayers will be with you."

General Ottman's adjunct, Captain Snyder, immediately stood up and said, "Attention!"

All the soldiers stood and came to attention.

Captain Snyder barked, "Dismissed!"

The civilian airplane with the Fantastic Six and their South African counterparts taxied down the runway at exactly 0400 hours. Their destination was an airport near a small safari camp. The Savuti South Camp was in the heart of Chobe National Park.

When they deplaned, they were directed to an all-terrain safari vehicle on the airfield. They got their gear placed on and in the vehicle and completed the journey to the Savuti Camp. Once in the camp, they went to the two tents that had been reserved for them and began to prepare to launch the rescue. The militia camp of the Inkatha Zulu splinter group where the girls were being held was approximately ninety miles to the northwest. It was not going to be an easy rescue.

They would leave the Savuti Camp at nine o'clock and drive through the wildlife-rich Chobe National Park, stopping to take photographs to avoid suspicion. They were sure there were many eyes ready to alert the militia camp that a rescue was being launched. They planned to arrive at the base of the mountain after nightfall, and they did not plan to ascend the mountain until very late at night so they could appear leisurely in their disguises.

CHAPTER 25

Vanholder and Moreno informed the White House, the South African Presidential House, and their respective staff persons who were privy to the information of all progress in the rescue effort.

Christian and O'Leary decided that the operation must be kept top secret. Everyone in the world expected some response, but no details were being given to the media. The media did not even know that the military camp had been located. Christian briefed Horace, but he did not give him all the details of the operation.

Winella Tocumba had served in the Inkatha Zulu Party Militia for five years. She was recruited by Betelema and was able to get a job at the US embassy in Pretoria shortly after the plan was devised to kidnap the ambassador's daughter. Horace and Beverly were not aware that one of the household staff was a plant and spy for Betelema.

Winella listened intently to all the conversations around the embassy while going about her household chores. No one suspected a thing. This night, while she served dinner with the household staff to Ambassador Davis and his wife, she listened as they discussed the impending rescue of their daughter and her friends.

Horace sat at the table with a slight frown on his face. He had been in deep thought about his conversation with Vanholder and had not decided whether or not to tell his wife because he did not want to raise false hopes. "Beverly, I spoke with Jon Vanholder this afternoon about Renée and her friends."

Beverly stopped eating and put down her fork.

He continued, "He told me they had located a camp in the Drakensberg Mountains of Natal Province where they are certain the girls are being held, and their intelligence has indicated that all of them are alive and well."

Beverly's eyes began to water but she made no audible sound.

"The US military and the South African military are preparing a rescue attempt, but he did not say when they would be ready or when the attempt was going to be made."

Beverly said, "Can they get them out without hurting them?"

"I'm sure they will do everything to ensure their safety. No details of the rescue were given to me. I don't really know when or how this rescue is going to be made. I just pray they do it soon, are successful, and Renée is brought home safe and unharmed to us."

Winella listened to the conversation while serving, but she gave no indication that she was paying attention. When she left the embassy, she went to the Inkatha headquarters building in Johannesburg and reported what she had heard to Betelema's lieutenant. This man reported only to Betelema; the top brass of the Inkatha Party, including its leader, Musa Goba, was not to know.

Betelema's man listened to the information and made some notes. Winella finished her report and left. Betelema's man went to the radio room, which was unoccupied, and radioed Betelema's headquarters at the camp in the mountains of Natal Province to report his findings. He reported all the information their spy in the US embassy had told him. He told Betelema to be aware and alert to the fact that they had been found and that a rescue of the captives was going to be attempted by the US and South African militaries. Betelema asked when this attempt was going to be made, but the informant said that the US ambassador did not know when this rescue operation was going to take place.

Betelema received this information and sat in deep thought at his desk. He thought about the impending rescue attempt and wondered if he had time to move to a new location. Preparations were being made at another deserted Inkatha campsite, but it would be at least another four days before it could be occupied. He did not expect to be found this soon. He had to take a chance and stay in this camp for a couple more days. He had to put more men and machinery to work in preparing the other camp.

Betelema called in his officers and said, "I have just heard from our headquarters in Johannesburg that our camp has been found by the South African and American reconnaissance airplanes. The American and South African armies are planning a rescue of hostages in the near future. We don't know when. We must be prepared for any rescue attempt made by them. I am certain they do not want to harm these girls, so they must surprise us. We know they are coming. We won't be surprised. We will be waiting for them.

If they do not make this attempt in the next couple of days, we will have time to move to the other camp—and we will not be here when they come. I want to make sure that they can't reach all the girls in one place if they attempt their rescue before we leave. For now, move two of the girls to the small barrack on the other side of the headquarters. We will separate them so it will make any attempt more difficult. Increase the number of guards and place sentries in the trees five miles from camp with two-way radios so that we may have plenty of advanced warning if a rescue operation comes up the mountain. A rescue would have to come by land in this rugged jungle. If they came by helicopter, we would hear them ten miles out."

The officers nodded and made sounds of agreement.

Betelema commanded, "Place all troops on alert—and double their ammunition ration." To carry out these orders immediately, militia officers quickly filed out of Betelema's makeshift headquarters.

Renée, Tina, Michelle, and Denise were awakened abruptly in the middle of the night. Tina and Denise were told to get their things together. They were moving. All the girls did as instructed. When they asked why they were being separated, they were given no answers.

This was going to change all their plans for an escape. They had been plotting for two days and were planning to make their getaway on Saturday night. They had already gotten a couple of heavy rocks discovered by the latrine and sneaked them into their barrack in their bath towels. They were going to use them to knock out the guards after they'd lured them into their barrack. The girls had even managed to steal the keys out of a Land Rover that was always parked near the shower and laundry area.

On Thursday afternoon, Michelle was washing her towel when she saw the keys in the ignition. She looked at the guards in the towers, and they were looking into the jungle. She checked to see if any other soldiers were watching, she quickly grabbed the keys, and placed them in her bra. The girls were hoping the last soldier to use the vehicle would be blamed for misplacing the keys.

They had studied the map that Renée had stolen and had worked out a route down the mountain. They would get past the guard towers by pretending to be soldiers taking prostitutes back to the village below in Botswana. They would take the uniforms off the two guards after they had knocked them out and then bind and gag them with pantyhose. They had prepared detailed plans for their escape—and now this.

Renée thought, *What triggered this? Did Betelema miss the map? Had someone suspected them of stealing the missing keys?*

Tina and Denise quickly packed their suitcases, and the guards took them.

Renée watched as they were taken away. She was terrified that something dreadful was going to happen to them. Were they going to be tortured or executed? Where were they taking them—and why?

The soldiers took them to another small barrack on the other side of headquarters.

Betelema entered the barrack where they had been taken and looked at them with a long agitated stare. "You are not to leave this side of the camp to visit your friends. Your guards will accompany you when you go to the bathroom or shower or wash your clothes. You will not communicate with your friends on the other side of the headquarters building. Is this understood?"

Tina and Denise nodded.

Betelema looked around the barrack one final time, turned, and walked out. He walked to the barrack where Renée and Michelle were being held and gave them the same instructions. Betelema knew that he and his troops must be very alert and ready for the rescue attempt. He did not want his mission to fail. He would definitely receive the wrath of Musa Goba and the other leaders for acting on his own if he failed, especially since he was working in conjunction with Higgs. *When I am successful with this mission, I will receive the praises of all the Inkatha Zulus, and Musa Goba and the other leaders will be very pleased. I will be promoted to an even more important position in our new independent Zulu homeland.*

Renée, Tina, Michelle, and Denise all felt doomed. Even though they could not communicate with each other, they all knew what the others felt. Their escape was foiled. They could not talk to one another. A new escape plan was impossible since they were now being guarded so closely.

CHAPTER 26

The rescue team reached the base of the mountain after a long day. The weather had been hot but not unbearable.

Colonel Tate was satisfied that their disguises had worked successfully. They had stopped a few times to take pictures of the wildlife and even visited with some of the locals they had encountered along the way. It was almost time to commence.

Colonel Tate reviewed the rescue plan with the Fantastic Six and the South African contingent before they started the ten-mile climb to the camp. Under cover of darkness, they had moved to the launching stage of their rescue effort. They had changed into their camouflage fatigues, assembled their weapons and night-vision gear, and checked their explosives and ammunition. They were ready to rescue the girls.

Donna Rhodes whispered, "Colonel, can we review the contingency plan for escape just in case something goes wrong with the operation?"

"If we are spotted before or after we rescue the hostages, we will assemble at the base of the camp, here." Colonel Tate pointed to a place on the map he'd spread out on the hood of their vehicle. "Then we will retreat at double time while returning fire if we are fired upon. Our objective is to return to our vehicle and get down the mountain."

"How about the helicopter rendezvous?" Bonita Hill asked. "Will that change?"

Colonel Tate answered, "Everyone should know the radio frequency to call in the helicopters in case one of us goes down. Harry has the radio, but you should all be prepared to call in backup from the helicopters."

Desmond Moussa asked, "Is there anything else you want Sofia and me to do from this point on other than provide more backup and support in a firefight?"

"No," said Colonel Tate. "Just be ready to fight like hell if that comes about."

Desmond and Sofia were no longer imitation safari guides. They were back to their roles as Special Forces soldiers. Major Hill, Sergeant Jackson, and Corporal Booker indicated that they had no further questions.

Corporal Harry Washington reached for his backpack of explosives, hoisted them onto his back, and picked up his M-16 automatic rifle. He didn't say a word. He just nodded. The Fantastic Six was ready to commence with the operation.

At two o'clock, the four-wheel-drive Hummer moved slowly up the mountain road toward the camp. Desmond drove with no lights on. The engine purred softly since it had been fitted with special mufflers for this operation. The night was clear, and the stars and moon were very bright. The visibility was pretty good. The plan was to drive within three miles of the camp, hide the vehicle, take the gear, and walk the rest of the way.

When they were about five miles from the camp, Colonel Tate had Desmond stop the vehicle. Something felt a little strange to him. He did not hear the birds and animal sounds he expected. He turned to Sofia and Desmond, and they had the same feeling.

After a few seconds, he decided it was too dangerous to continue in the vehicle. Colonel Tate decided to begin the hike from that point.

They hid the vehicle in the trees and brush and began to hike up the mountain.

According to the map, they were five and a half miles from the camp. So far, so good! They moved quietly through the jungle with their night-vision goggles. They passed monkeys and birds and even a large snake, but none made much noise. The jungle was thick and the climb difficult, but the rescue team expected this. They could not hack their way through because that would make too much noise.

Tarik took point about ten feet ahead of the rest of the team. Eddie brought up the rear, always looking back, in case someone or something tried to come upon them from the rear. The climb was slow and deliberate. They wanted to reach the camp undetected. That was more important than the time they arrived there. The objective was to use cover of darkness, and they had plenty of time before sunrise. They would make up any time getting back to the bottom of the mountain after they rescued the hostages.

The night was very still except for the rustling of the trees, the calls of birds, and the sounds of jungle animals. They had seen plenty of wildlife on the photographic safari and knew there was large wildlife in the mountains too, but they had not encountered any leopards, lions, or water buffalo. They continued their ascent up the mountain.

Tarik signaled for everyone to stop and be quiet. He had heard something in the trees that sounded like a human voice. He wanted to check it out before the rest of the team moved forward. He inched his way forward, being careful not to make a sound. He reached into his backpack and pulled out a heat-detecting device, which could detect a warm-blooded being at night. He looked through it after he cradled his heavy machine gun in his left arm. He scanned the treetops and saw the outline of a man in a tree fifty feet to his left. He continued to scan the treetops and saw another figure a hundred feet to his right.

He put on his night-vision glasses again to see if they could be seen. Since he knew exactly where they were, he could see them.

Tarik inched his way back to the rescue squad and reported to Colonel Tate what he had seen.

Tate realized they had to locate all the treetop sentries and neutralize them quickly and quietly. He explained the situation and ordered the team to remain where they were. Moving in perfectly silent stealth, he and Tarik arrived at the position where Tarik had spotted the sentries. With their night-vision goggles and the heat-detection devices, they were able to spot five sentries in the trees. Colonel Tate and Tarik were undetected and were sure they had located all the sentries.

Marvin and Tarik returned to the group.

Marvin whispered, "There are five guards up in the trees. We can't get past them without being spotted. We have to neutralize them. It's going to have to be done really quietly. We can't shoot them down with our rifles. Bonita, you're going to have to take them out with your bow and arrows."

Major Hill immediately placed her carrying case on the ground and pulled out her archery equipment. She put on the night-vision goggles and followed Colonel Tate and Tarik to the first target. The others stayed behind.

The sentries were fanned out over a 150-yard area not far from the road. Bonita had to shoot them with enough force to knock them out of the trees while Tarik and Marvin would have to move into position to break their falls to keep them from making noise as they hit the ground.

Bonita waited for the other team members to get into position under the tree where the first sentry was posted. She took aim at the target. She could see him clearly through her night-vision goggles. The militia sentry never knew what hit him. Suddenly, he was struck in the upper right shoulder with such a force that he was on the ground before he could utter a sound.

Tarik and Marvin held his mouth and hit him in the head with a large handgun, rendering him unconscious. Marvin quickly cut the sleeve off the sentry's shirt with a large knife and gagged him. He used the soldier's belt to tie his hands. He cut his other sleeve and tied his legs. Tarik pulled the arrow from his shoulder. It was a deep flesh wound. He would live, but the soldier wasn't going anywhere anytime soon. He was going to be out for hours.

Bonita took aim at the next sentry and let her arrow fly. This time, it found its mark in the middle of the sentry's chest. The sentry was dead when he hit the ground. They moved on to the next, and then the next, and then the next. Three were still alive, and two were dead. None made any noise and would not until after this operation was over. Tarik, Marvin, and Bonita returned to the others, and they continued up the mountain. They were just three miles from the camp.

The forward sentries of the militia camp had been neutralized. Their radio communications equipment had been confiscated. Desmond had the equipment in his possession in case there was some communication that called for a response, especially if the communication was in Zulu.

After ten minutes, the rescue team saw the flickering of light from the camp. They halted and dropped their gear after they saw the guard towers.

Colonel Tate gave everyone five minutes to catch their breath before they began to implement the most critical part of the rescue of the hostages

"Ready? Go," he said.

Colonel Tate and Tarik moved forward to look at the camp with their night-vision binoculars. Upon reaching a spot one hundred feet from the first guard tower, they found a point from which they could see the entire camp. It was on a little knoll at the top of the mountain. It looked just like their training village. The camp was awash with light, and the soldiers were obviously on full alert. Some were behind bunkers; others were busily moving around the camp in preparation for an attack. The rescue team was expected!

Colonel Tate and Tarik looked at each other with the same concerned expression. This was going to call for a change in plans. They had come too far to not attempt to get the girls out of the camp. They knew they couldn't just sneak into the camp, find the girls, come back out, and go down the mountain. This called for a whole new plan.

The two men made their way back to their comrades and described the situation.

Colonel Tate said, "The camp is just like the mock camp we built at Fort Bragg. The difference is these guys are on full alert. Somebody tipped them. They're expecting us. We have to make some changes in our plans, but we're still going to get those girls out."

The other team members looked at each other questioningly.

Tate said, "Here is what we're going to do." He began to outline the modifications in the rescue plan, drawing diagrams on the ground and on the map. They discussed the changes in low whispers until everybody understood their new assignments. The new strategy was formed in ten minutes.

When they understood and were ready to go, Colonel Tate gave the order to commence the rescue operation. The Fantastic Six plus two were now as fully prepared as they were going to be to carry forth the rescue operation.

Donna Rhodes, a top marksperson with an M-16 rapid-firing automatic, moved into position. At the drop of Colonel Tate's hand, she fired her weapon, which had been fitted with a barrel silencer.

The first tower guard dropped without a sound. Within two seconds, a second shot was fired, and the other guard in the first tower went down. Both guards had been neutralized without a sound. Sergeant Eddie Jackson quickly ran through the trees to the guard tower, climbed up, and made sure it was secured.

Immediately after downing the second guard at the first tower, Donna turned her attention to the second guard tower. Within five seconds of shooting the guards in the first tower, she shot the first guard in the second tower. A few seconds later, she eliminated the second guard in the tower.

Tarik was already moving into position as Donna was shooting, and he scurried up the tower quietly. One guard was still alive, but Tarik hit him with the butt of his machine gun. The towers were secured in only twelve seconds.

The lights on the towers were still on and in position to survey the camp and the surrounding jungle. Everything appeared normal to the soldiers in the camp. It was about two and a half hours before sunrise. The rescue mission had to move rapidly.

Corporal Harry Washington, the explosives expert, moved around the outside of the camp to the barracks at both ends. The tower guards would have seen him if they had not been neutralized. He moved from the trees and crawled under the first barrack. He looked through a window to see if it was occupied, but it was empty.

The soldiers were all in the camp compound preparing their defense.

Harry placed C-4 under the first barrack and moved cautiously behind the other barracks through the trees, making sure he was not seen. He continued to the far side of the camp to a second barrack where he looked for the girls and then planted more C-4. He set the timing devices to detonate the explosives in ten minutes.

Donna and Bonita moved around the back of each barrack very quickly and surreptitiously. They had to locate the girls before the explosives went off. Everyone in the rescue effort was synchronized, moving silently from barrack to barrack through the trees behind the camp. They heard voices nearby and spotted a small barrack that was being guarded by two soldiers.

Bonita signaled to Donna that it must be where the girls were being held. Not a word was spoken. They looked in a little window and saw Michelle through an open door to the bathroom. This was it!

They had to eliminate the guards without a sound. They made a little noise behind the barrack, and a guard went to investigate. The guard figured anyone approaching the camp would have been spotted by the forward sentries in the trees or the soldiers in the guard towers, but he was cautious nevertheless. When he came around to the back of the barrack, he saw nothing and thought it must have been an animal. He turned to go back to the front of the barrack.

At that moment, Bonita grabbed his feet from her position under the barrack and pulled them out from under him. At that same instant, Donna quickly rolled out from under the building and knocked him unconscious with her gun. They dragged him under the barrack. There was almost complete silence.

The second guard called out, "What did you see?"

There was no response.

He called again with no response. "Is something wrong? I'm coming to check it out."

At that instant, Bonita and Donna came around the corner. Bonita drew her army knife and threw it before the militia guard could react. The knife found its target, striking him in the shoulder. He fell in front of the door, and Donna quickly hit him in the head with her gun to be sure he remained down. He would be out for hours. At least they didn't have to kill him. The two women moved quickly and carefully and darted through the front door.

Renée and Michelle almost screamed when they saw the two black women in camouflage khakis with US flag patches on their shoulders. They were so incredibly excited and stunned that their mouths and their eyes were wide open.

Renée had a million questions running through her head. *Is this really happening? Do they know where Tina and Denise are? What do we do now?*

Three minutes had passed. They had seven minutes to find the other girls and return to the rendezvous point. There was no time for niceties.

Bonita whispered, "Stay calm. We're US Army rescue squad."

Donna asked, "What are your names?"

Renée answered, "I'm Renée, and she's Michelle. How many of you are there?"

"Where are the other two girls being kept?" Donna asked, ignoring Renée's question.

"They are in the second barrack on the other side of the largest barrack," Renée said. "A barrack like this one. They have two guards at the front door all the time. What happened to our guards? How did you get past them?"

Bonita and Donna continued to ignore the questions.

No one inside the camp had missed the guards in front of the barrack where Renée and Michelle were being held. The four women crouched down, quickly exited the barrack's front door, and ran behind it.

Donna told Bonita to take Renée and Michelle to the rendezvous point, and she would go forward to rescue the other two girls. Bonita nodded and told Renée and Michelle to stay down and follow her. She took them through the trees to the rendezvous point where Colonel Tate, Desmond, Sofia, and Harry were waiting.

Donna made her way through the trees to the other side of the headquarters building. From that vantage point, she could see two guards in front of the barrack where Denise and Tina were being held. Many other soldiers were nearby. There was a bunker only twenty feet away, and there was a lot of activity around what appeared to be a supply barrack next to the barrack where the girls were being held. There was no way that Donna was going to take these guards out the way that she and Bonita had taken out the other guards. She needed a diversion. It was two minutes away from detonation time. She looked at her gun and decided to wait for the explosions before getting the girls.

Donna moved forward just behind the barrack where the girls were being held. She was careful to remain hidden and prayed that both girls were inside. She did not want to take the chance of being seen in order to take a look in the window in the back, and she stayed put.

Two minutes seemed like an eternity. There was activity and preparation all over the camp, but the rescue team had not been detected. The militia radio dispatcher from the headquarters barrack had called out to the forward sentries in Zulu. Desmond had answered that all was okay. The dispatcher was satisfied and said he would check back later.

Two gigantic explosions rocked the camp at both ends when the C-4 blew up the barracks. Pandemonium broke out, and soldiers fired in the direction of the explosions.

Donna quickly moved in from her position and shot both guards as they turned to face her with their rifles.

Tarik and Eddie fired the machine guns from the towers. The rest of the rescue team fired from ground positions in the trees.

Harry threw hand grenades. They wanted to give the impression that they were a full battalion or several squadrons attacking the camp.

Donna lunged through the unlocked door of the barrack. Tina and Denise had turned the table over and were hiding behind it. Donna quickly identified herself. "We've come to get you guys out of here! Keep your heads and your butts down and follow me."

The girls were scared to death after hearing all the explosions and the guns firing all around them. They wanted to ask a million questions, but they decided to just do as they were told.

Donna started to go through the door, but she changed her mind when she saw bullets flying everywhere. The barrack had a large back window. She quickly took a chair, broke the window, grabbed a couple of sheets, and put them over the sill after clearing off the broken glass. She climbed out the window and helped Tina and Denise climb out. They ran toward the rendezvous position, keeping low and behind the trees.

Eddie and Tarik continued to fire from the towers, and the other members of the rescue team continued to fire from the trees while Donna ran to the rendezvous position with the girls.

Renée saw Tina and Denise running toward her and let out a little scream. Renée, Tina, Michelle, and Denise hugged each other, staying low behind the trees. They were frightened to death but also very excited. Two minutes were left for everyone to return to the rendezvous position to begin the retreat down the mountain.

Colonel Tate asked for the radio. He called for helicopter gunships to cover them once they got to the lowlands.

Eddie and Tarik looked at their synchronized watches and realized it was time to move to the rendezvous positions. They put on their gloves and slid down the side of the tower ladders simultaneously. They made their way quickly to the rendezvous point. The ground fire continued, and a continuous barrage of hand grenades was being thrown into the camp. The other explosives that Harry had planted went off to ensure that the camp remained under siege and to force the soldiers to defend the camp from their bunkers.

Everyone in the rescue operation moved to the rendezvous point "Let's move out," Colonel Tate ordered.

They retreated toward the vehicle, and Harry and Tarik took up rear positions. Tarik picked up his big machine gun and continuously sprayed the camp with bullets while retreating. Harry used a grenade launcher to fire hand grenades into the camp. The team was in full retreat. The whole rescue operation took only fifteen minutes.

Betelema stumbled out of the headquarters and ran to the nearest bunker when the explosions went off. He yelled orders to his soldiers to return fire. They fired blindly at the flashes of light they could see coming from the trees. The gunfire from the towers was pinning them down.

Betelema realized that the firing had stopped coming from different areas in the trees and the towers even though bullets were still flying and explosions were still rocking the camp. He knew the attacking force must be in retreat or were preparing for an assault. He crouched down and ran to the nearest barrack where he had been holding the girls. It was empty. The back window had been broken out. He knew before he reached it that the other barrack was also empty. He returned to the bunker and told his men to cease firing. The firing from the trees had stopped.

Betelema ordered his men to pursue the attackers in a full battle assault. The soldiers then sprang into action immediately.

Tarik and Harry retreated along the road leading from the camp. They had to give the others time to travel to the vehicle. Harry planted explosives on the road that would detonate when a vehicle drove over a line that he had strung across the road. He set them about every hundred yards. They could hear the trucks coming and realized that the jungle was also full of pursuing troops. Everybody in the rescue team had to keep moving rapidly.

The rescue team and the girls were running through the trees and bushes as fast as they could. They were getting scratched up, but no one cared. Their only thoughts were of getting off the mountain. Not a word was spoken as everyone continued the descent.

They heard the pursuing soldiers moving down the mountain behind them. There was a loud explosion on the road behind them, and a reddish-orange fireball could be seen as they looked over their shoulders.

Tarik and Harry knew that a truck or jeep must have run over one of the explosives they left behind.

"That'll slow them down because they'll be more cautious looking out for other explosives," Harry said.

The jungle was alive with pursuing troops, and they were closing in rapidly. The retreating rescue party could hear the troops coming closer. Without warning, grenades began to explode all around them. The militia soldiers were using grenade launchers randomly. The team had another mile to go.

Tarik and Harry had caught up with the rest of the team. They had stopped firing at the chasing soldiers because they did not want to give away their exact location. There were so many soldiers with so many weapons that it didn't make sense to fire at them. If they stopped to fight, they would be slaughtered. They had to run.

The girls were keeping up with the fast pace, but they had no choice. They were all in good physical shape, and their adrenaline was pumping.

Harry stopped momentarily to set more booby traps and caught up with the others. He hoped they would slow down the rapidly advancing troops.

They finally reached the vehicle, threw aside the branches, and leaped inside.

Desmond took the wheel and started the vehicle. He backed it out and drove onto the road. It was pitch black except for the stars and the moon above. He had to turn on the lights. He gunned the engine and started driving as fast as he could down the mountain road.

Tarik was in the back with a mounted machine gun. The others were seated in various positions in the special nine-passenger vehicle. Suddenly, a fast-moving truck with soldiers and a mounted machine gun was right behind them. Following that armored vehicle was another truck loaded with soldiers. The mounted machine gun in the armored truck opened fire.

Tarik returned the fire as the chase continued.

Desmond began to go faster down the mountain road.

The girls screamed but got themselves under control when they dropped to the floor of the vehicle. The two trucks behind them were getting closer. The ride was rough and bumpy, and bullets were flying all around them.

Renée was shaking.

Tina had begun to cry. Renée hugged her and could see the terror in her friends' eyes. She started to pray silently from the floor of the vehicle.

Tarik, Donna, Harry, Eddie, Bonita, Sofia, and Colonel Tate fired back at the trucks chasing them. The gun battle raged on. The winding road made it almost impossible for either side to hit anyone.

Renée wondered if they were going to survive.

They were five miles from the lowlands.

"That helicopter had better be there," Colonel Tate yelled.

The pursuing trucks were gaining on them. The only advantages they had were that the vehicle had a steel cover and four-wheel drive. As the other vehicles got closer, with about three miles to go, Colonel

Tate yelled, "Desmond, turn off the road. We're going to four-wheel it through the jungle."

Desmond turned into the jungle. The militia trucks followed, blasting away at them. After a few hundred yards, the jungle thickened. The four-wheel drive vehicle slowed down considerably but continued to plow its way through. The pursuing trucks followed for a few hundred yards. When they could not go any deeper into the jungle, the troops jumped out of the trucks and continued the pursuit on foot.

Betelema came up in another truck with more troops and began to direct the pursuit. The four-wheel drive had slowed considerably in the thick jungle. They were just a couple thousand yards ahead of the soldiers pursuing on foot. With just two miles to go, the four-wheel drive vehicle came to a halt.

Everyone immediately jumped out of the vehicle and ran down the mountain

Tarik and Harry took up the rear with their machine gun and explosives. The soldiers were gaining. There were fifty or sixty of them. They found the Hummer and realized the rescue team was on foot again.

Betelema sent about ten soldiers back to their vehicles to go down the mountain road to the lowlands to reach the area where the rescue team must come out of the jungle.

Colonel Tate kept his team and the girls moving through the thick brush. They could hear the soldiers behind them. They weren't that far away. Their only chance of escape was to reach the lowlands and the waiting helicopters. They had about a mile to go.

The two vehicles sent to intercept the rescue team drove rapidly down the mountain and turned along the foothills to the place they knew the rescue team would come out of the jungle. They turned their vehicles toward the jungle so they could turn their lights on the rescue team and blast them.

The soldiers with Betelema heard the rescue team breaking through the bush ahead. They began to fire blindly in that direction. The rescue team members turned periodically and returned fire equally blindly in the hope of slowing down the soldiers. They could finally see the end of the brush and trees and knew they had only a few more feet to the clearing.

When they burst through the last of the foliage into abrupt openness, lights filled the darkness with such brightness that it stunned and blinded them. They froze for a long moment and then dove to the ground.

Oh Lord, this is it, Colonel Tate thought.

The soldiers were in front and behind them. They were doomed. They prepared to fight or—if given the chance—they would stand up and be taken as hostages along with the girls they were trying to rescue. It looked as though their rescue efforts had ultimately failed.

After what seemed like an eternity, a loud roar filled the air, and bright lights came over a hill just two hundred yards away. Three helicopters were approaching with guns blasting away, shooting at the two trucks and the soldiers manning them. A rocket was launched, and the smaller truck blew up. Another rocket was fired, and the other truck followed the same fate. The soldiers ran as the helicopters mowed them down.

The soldiers in the jungle saw the explosions, heard the helicopters, and took cover. The two helicopter gunships began spraying automatic weapon fire into the trees behind the rescue team and the girls.

Colonel Tate signaled his team and the girls to follow him to the rescue helicopter that had landed. They ran toward the helicopter.

Its blades were turning so rapidly that the force almost knocked them over, but they managed to get to the open door.

Tarik and Eddie pushed the girls inside while the crew helped pull them in. The rescue team piled into the helicopter, and it was airborne again. The Fantastic Six, with their South African Special Forces companions, had succeeded.

Renée could not believe it. She screamed, "We're safe!"

The four friends started hugging each other and the rescuers excitedly. They were yelling their thanks to their rescuers and celebrating, relieved that they were finally free.

Betelema kept his troops down low and didn't try to engage the superior firepower of the helicopter gunships, which kept up the barrage until the rescue helicopter was out of danger.

The pilots continued up the mountain to the empty camp and leveled it. When the camp was totally destroyed, the helicopters turned around and returned to the airbase in Durban.

CHAPTER 27

Betelema knew he was in deep trouble. He returned to his mountain camp to find that it was in ruins. The camp was leveled and on fire. Nothing was left standing. He had failed. He had undertaken the mission on his own without the knowledge of Musa Goba or the Inkatha Zulu governing council. He had cooperated with Higgs and his ultra-right-wing splinter group to advocate a Volkstaat. This was a disaster, probably treason. He would have to leave the country, but first he had to address what was left of his troops.

Betelema assembled his militia in the bombed-out camp and gazed at his beaten troops. They had been loyal to him. "Men, we have tried to serve our people in this mission to give our leaders leverage to negotiate with the ANC government of Mandela. We have not succeeded. We cannot return to our Inkatha bases or to our homes." He paused, fighting to keep his composure and show strength in the face of defeat. "Our leaders in the council will consider us all insubordinate soldiers. I do not want you to be persecuted for my failure. Many of our comrades have been lost or wounded in this effort. I am very sorry for this and especially sorry that we did not succeed. I thank you for your loyalty and your service for the Inkatha Zulu people. You must not return to your families. Leave them for now and cross the border into Zimbabwe to avoid arrest by the South African government and the wrath of the Inkatha Zulu Council. I honor you, all of you. We must now bury our dead, attend to the wounded, take whatever is salvageable, and leave."

It was dawn, and Betelema knew that he owed it to his lifelong friend, Musa Goba, to explain why he had gone against his wishes and those of the Inkatha Zulu Council. Even though he knew he might be captured, he decided to go to the Inkatha Zulu homeland area in Natal Province to speak to Musa Goba. Since his reason for disobeying the council and acting on his own was for the uplifting of his people, he was certain that Musa Goba would understand and forgive him. He felt that Musa Goba would plead his case before the council. Betelema would have to leave the country after that because he knew the South African government was already seeking him.

Betelema drove through Botswana to the Inkatha Zulu headquarters. He entered the area later that night and knew that Musa Goba had already been informed of the failed operation.

Betelema drove to Musa Goba's house, parked his jeep, and looked around. Six men armed with automatic rifles were guarding the house. *The guards will know me; after all, I am the highest-ranking officer in the Inkatha Zulu militia.*

Betelema walked to the front of the house. The first guard approached him, weapon at the ready, and demanded that he identify himself. Betelema did so, including his rank.

The guard recognized him, lowered his weapon, and saluted. "What is the nature of your business, sir?" asked the guard. Apparently the Inkatha Zulu Council had given no arrest order for Betelema yet.

"I wish to speak with President Musa Goba," Betelema said.

The guard told him to wait and went into the house. The other guards who were watching and listening to the entire proceeding continued to watch Betelema. They were aware of what had happened the night before.

The first guard returned and beckoned Betelema to enter the house.

Musa Goba was waiting in his living room. The two old friends looked at each other for a long moment. Finally, Musa Goba dismissed the guard and gestured for Betelema to sit.

Betelema said, "Hello, my president and friend."

Musa Goba nodded.

Betelema continued, "I know, through your network of informants, that you are aware of the many events of the past few weeks and especially of the occurrences last night and early this morning."

Musa Goba nodded again.

"You know I have always been loyal to the Inkatha Zulu Party," Betelema said. "I wanted to give you my explanation and report in person. I felt you deserved that from me. I know that I went against specific orders from the council after you had given your word to participate in the elections. However, I thought it would increase the Inkatha Party's bargaining power if we had some leverage with the elected Parliament in their rewriting of the constitution. I believe if I had succeeded, we would have had that power. I did not want to work with the Afrikaners, but I needed help to implement my plan—and they also wanted leverage for their Volkstaat. I did not feel their objectives interfered with ours. I have failed, and I have lost many of my men in the process. I have disobeyed orders, and I know I am a sought-after fugitive of the South African government. I was trying to help my people and our cause. I am only sorry that I failed."

Musa Goba said, "My friend, I understand your motivation, but as is true in any well-organized party, there must be a chain of command. In the Inkatha Zulu Party, we have a very well-defined order of command. Even though you are the highest-ranking member of our military army, you must adhere to the orders and mandates of the council. I, as president, also must follow the dictates of the council, even though I have the leeway to make many decisions without prior consultation. You, however, were specifically ordered to not carry out any action against the new South African government—and you did. Who were your Afrikaner accomplices?"

Betelema gave him information about Higgs and the Volker group. He told him he did not know the hijackers, but he could identify them. He tried to explain to Musa Goba that he needed them to pull off the hijacking.

"You know I cannot accept this explanation as an excuse to work with one of our most revolting enemies," Musa Goba replied. "You will be arrested when you leave my house. The council has decided to try you for insubordination and treason. I personally am very sorry, my friend, but there is nothing I can do about this. It has already been decided. Your travel from Botswana to Natal was monitored until you arrived here. You were allowed to come to see me when it became obvious that was your intention."

Betelema and Musa Goba stood and embraced. They had been close friends since boyhood. Betelema took a step back and saluted his president. When he left the house, council guards were waiting for him outside and placed him under arrest.

The council had not decided whether or not they would turn him over to the new South African government. That would be decided at the Inkatha Council trial.

Musa Goba hesitated for a moment. He was very sad and did not look forward to what he had to do, but he walked toward his telephone. He slowly dialed. "This is Musa Goba. May I speak with President Mandela? This is regarding the kidnapping of the US ambassador's daughter." There was a long pause.

"Hello, Mr. Goba," President Mandela said.

"President Mandela, Betelema did, indeed, come to my home to confess his participation in the kidnapping." Musa Goba sighed. "He also was working with the Afrikaner, Higgs, who was intricately involved in the hijacking of the plane."

When their talk ended, Musa Goba hung up the phone and placed his face in his hands. He could not help his longtime friend anymore.

Betelema went before the Inkatha Council for trial. It was decided that he be turned over to the South African government authorities.

The South African Intelligence Agency interrogated Betelema, and he was very cooperative. They obtained information about Higgs' role in the hijacking and kidnapping. It was decided that the government would arrest Higgs and disband his organization, which was not going to be an easy undertaking.

Higgs' group was armed and located in the ultraconservative area of western Transvaal. This rural area was made up of small farming towns where white extremists had vowed to wage guerrilla warfare against the government until it gave them a separate white homeland, a Volkstaat.

Higgs's organization headquarters was located near the town of Oakney. He had the support of several other ultraconservative organizations.

CHAPTER 28

Renée looked out the window at the airport landing area. The helicopter carrying the rescued girls, the Fantastic Six rescue team, and their South African comrades landed at an air force base outside of Pretoria. The rescue had been a successful but harrowing experience for both the professional soldiers and the girls.

"Thank you so much for saving us", Renee repeated with deep sincerity but felt that the expression was surely insufficient. The other girls echoed her sentiments. They were all still shaken by their harrowing experience. They realized that the rescue could have been a deadly failure if the helicopters had not shown up when they did.

Renée said, "We didn't know what was going to happen to us. We know you risked your lives to help us."

After a brief exchange of hugs, thank-yous, and stories about the Fantastic Six and their South African Special Forces rescuers, South African Air Force personnel escorted the girls into a nearby building. They were briefly greeted by the base commander, taken to a waiting ambulance, and transported to the base hospital.

Rene attempted levity to the moment by not-too seriously asking, "Are you guys okay? I know we all got scratched up, but nobody got shot……right?!"

The girls started talking all at the same time.

Tina exclaimed, "Not shot—but scared to death! I never ran that fast in my whole life. Can you believe that those fools were shooting at us? I almost died when those truck lights came on. Where are they taking us?"

The ambulance reached the base hospital and the talking stopped.

Arriving in a separate military vehicle, the Fantastic Six walked into the building with Desmond and Sofia.

"Congratulations on the success of your mission," said a passing soldier.

They were professional soldiers, but they had never had another combat experience where they'd come so close to death. It had been a seriously intense situation. They hugged each other like rookies. Donna, Bonita, and Sofia hugged each other and visibly teared. Even the men were fighting back tears. They were all excited and thankful to God to have made it back to the base unharmed. It had been a great rescue!

Colonel Tate brought the celebration to a halt. "Listen up," he said. "We have to report to the debriefing room to make our report. I just received word that Major General Moreno and Mr. Vanholder are waiting for us. Let's move out."

Major General Moreno and Jon Vanholder had already gotten the news from the radio dispatcher and the base commander that the operation had been a success and that all had returned safely. Moreno had relayed the information to the Pentagon, and they had notified the State Department and the White House. He needed to get a detailed report from Colonel Tate and the other soldiers so that he could prepare a comprehensive report for General Genoa Sheppard, the chairman of the Joint Chiefs of Staff. General Sheppard would prepare the final report to be presented to the Secretary of State Christian and President Benson.

Colonel Tate and the rescue team were taken to the headquarters building where Major General Moreno was waiting with Jon Vanholder. The rescuers were escorted to the debriefing room. When they entered, they saluted the two men and their staffs. The room looked like a classroom except there were about thirty chairs in rows instead of desks. A stenographer transcribed the proceedings from behind a desk. General Moreno and Jon Vanholder stood in front of the room. After cordial greetings and congratulations for the rescue team, the Fantastic Six began the debriefing.

A team of military and civilian doctors from the US and South Africa was waiting for the girls at the base hospital. They were to have thorough physical and psychological examinations after a joyful reunion with their parents.

When Renée saw her parents, she started to cry. All the parents and daughters embraced and wept. The girls talked excitedly to their parents, and the parents spoke excitedly to them, the girls about their awful experience and the parents of their fears and anxieties.

Beverly hugged Renée tightly and said, "Thank God you are safe. Your dad and I were so worried that we were just numb. We prayed and did not give up hope that you would be rescued unharmed. And here you are, thank God. We love you so much."

All the parents were hugging and celebrating the rescue of their daughters. It was a happy, tearful, and exhilarating reunion.

Beverly said, "Michelle, Denise, and Tina's parents are our houseguests at the embassy. The US government flew them all out a few days ago."

After an hour, the medical director of the hospital announced that the girls had to leave for their examinations. They would have to stay in the hospital for at least two days. After more embraces between daughters and parents, the girls left the room with nurses.

CHAPTER 29

President Benson and President Mandela were informed of the details of the hijacking, kidnapping, and rescue. They also had been given the details of the treatment of the girls while in captivity, which had been obtained during the debriefing.

Musa Goba and President Mandela met to discuss the past couple of weeks.

President Mandela said, "Thank you, Mr. Goba, for coming to my office to meet with me. The events that have occurred with the kidnapping of the US ambassador's daughter have made the bringing together of all factions of the South African citizens more difficult. We are trying to move forward in South Africa and this kind of activity is just an obstacle to our progress."

Musa Goba replied, "Mr. Mandela, even though my fellow Zulu tribesmen and I did not support your election—and we are still opposed to it—we did not sanction the hijacking and kidnapping. Betelema carried out his plan without the knowledge of the Inkatha Freedom Party council. Further, Betelema has been turned over to the South African authorities and he has given them information about who his accomplices were."

President Mandela replied, "Thank you, Mr. Goba, for coming forth with this information and for turning over Betelema to be tried by the South African government." He knew it was an endorsement of his new presidency and government. He continued trying to convince Musa Goba to join his new cabinet.

President Mandela met with his top civilian and military officials and said, "We must now plan a strategy to arrest Higgs and the members of his organization and bring them in for trial for the hijacking of SSA Flight 283 and the kidnapping of the US ambassador's daughter and her friends. Devise a plan and bring it back to this committee by tomorrow morning at seven o'clock."

Higgs had a following of approximately 650 men and women. His group was well armed, and most members had military or police training. The organization ran a small radio station at their headquarters that spewed neo-Nazi propaganda and racial hate. Barbed wire and bunkers surrounded their headquarters near Oakney, and they were willing to fight to the death to protect Higgs and the other hijackers.

The arrest operation was going to be the first big test of Mandela's presidential power over the South African military and police authorities. The military and police officials were primarily white men who had been the enforcers and protectors of apartheid.

President Mandela met with his chief of staff, chief military commander, and director of internal security to discuss the capture and arrest of Higgs and the other hijackers so they could be brought to trial. He knew the risk of a military operation in western Transvaal and Orange Free State. If the other pro-apartheid Afrikaner organizations joined in a military resistance with them, it could escalate into a civil war. President Mandela also knew that the Inkatha Freedom Party, the ANC, and the newly elected democratic government of South Africa could not allow the kidnapping of the ambassador's daughter to go unpunished. It would not sit well with the Americans, the rest of the Western world, or the black African nations.

President Mandela convinced his military commanders and key political officials that these people must be brought to justice in order for the new government to be accepted by people throughout the world. This was especially true for the Americans on whose trade and goodwill the new South African economy would be so heavily dependent. All the authorities involved in this operation agreed that Higgs had to be brought to justice.

Higgs knew that President Mandela and other government officials knew that his organization was responsible for the hijacking and kidnapping along with the renegade Inkatha group that Betelema commanded. He was awaiting a response from the South African government. They were making preparations to defend themselves.

Higgs was trying to convince the other ultraconservative white organizations to join him. Hourly broadcasts were being made to enlist the help and allegiance of the other organizations. Many of the pro-Volkstat separatist groups were considering his solicitation, but they realized that the government would be coming at them with a large, modern military force. They did not want to entertain that kind of confrontation.

President Madiba, as he was called by many of his countrymen, went on the radio and television to inform the country of the government's intent to bring the hijackers and kidnappers to justice. He appealed to all other groups to not take a part in this situation and make it their fight. He asked that all factions of the country begin to cooperate with his new government so that the country might move forward toward a level of prosperity that could be enjoyed by all the people of South Africa. He told them that the entire world was watching them.

The White Afrikaner Alliance met to discuss their position without Higgs—and then with Higgs. They decided that he should have discussed the operation with them before undertaking it and agreed that he had placed them all in very dangerous positions before they were ready for a confrontation with the military of South Africa. Higgs was on his own!

Chapter 30

Higgs told his organization about the decision made by the White Afrikaner Alliance. His organization decided to take a stand to protect Higgs, the men involved in the hijacking, and their territory.

Higgs sat in his office at the Freedom Alliance headquarters. He was very worried about the ensuing events. He thought, *I believed that all we did would succeed. The Americans and their rescue team fooled us. I should not have trusted Betelema to get this right. I should have done the whole operation myself.* He pounded the desk. *Damn it.* He knew the government forces were going to come after him and his followers, and they had to be prepared. *We are going to give them a hell of a fight.* He stood up and went to direct his people in the preparation for the inevitable assault.

In addition to the 650 in his group, there were approximately 350 sympathizers from other Afrikaner organizations who had come to fight to the death, if necessary, against the new government.

Preparations were continuously being made for the expected assault. Trenches were dug around the compound, and new bunkers were erected. Heavy antitank guns were mounted and waiting. Most of the men were recently discharged soldiers and policemen—trained fighters. This was not going to be a surprise hit-and-run attack in the middle of the night.

South Africa probably had the best-equipped and best-trained military on the African continent. The military strategists met to determine how they could attack this situation with as few casualties as possible. They wanted it to be a quick and successful operation that would be a lesson for anyone who wished to wage war against the new government.

President Mandela knew that the planned attack posed a delicate and difficult situation for the white South African generals. They were going to have to wage war against fellow white South Africans for a new black president and a majority-black Parliament. It was a rude ushering in of a new era and the ultimate test of the power and legitimacy of his presidency.

The South African military was integrated, and many of the new members were from what had been the guerrilla forces of the ANC. The operation had to be carried out by predominately white officers and black troops.

After the top-secret military plan was devised, the generals presented it to Jon Vanholder and his strategists for approval. A lengthy presentation and discussion took place at the military headquarters in Pretoria. Many important aspects of the operation were debated and changed. All salient parts of the plan were reviewed numerous times until every point was agreed upon. The military had made its decision to back the new president and move South Africa forward to a true democratic society.

CHAPTER 31

At three o'clock in the morning, an airplane flying at thirty thousand feet sent a bomb with a guidance device crashing into the main generator of the Freedom Alliance military headquarters compound. All lights went off!

The underground gasoline-driven emergency generators were turned on immediately. There was enough gasoline to keep them running for up to six months. Ten minutes later, another bomb hit the water tank, which came tumbling down, nearly drowning some of the men in the trenches. The compound also had backup water supplies. The water supply from the wells they dug had underground piping as well.

Even though he knew it was coming, Higgs was startled by the attack. He had fallen asleep at his desk. He ran out of his office and yelled, "Get ready. The assault is coming."

The compound was on high alert. Higgs and his followers dug in, awaiting the ground assault.

From ten miles away, the South African military sent a barrage of shells into the compound. The generals wanted to drive most of the rebels underground or into their bunkers.

Reconnaissance flights had taken high-resolution photographs of the compound. It was obvious that the attack was expected. The camp was prepared; a mere bombardment was not going to make

Higgs and his followers give up easily. However, the first attack was a surprise to Higgs and his military strategists.

While the shells were being lobbed, high-flying bombers dropped five-hundred-pound bombs on the compound, knocking out all the big guns. The men in the trenches retreated to underground positions or into the bunkers.

Higgs and his troops had not fired a shot because they couldn't see anybody, and the shells were coming from so many directions. Jon Vanholder and his strategists had devised a psychological warfare strategy that was designed to confuse the enemy without inflicting a great number of casualties. The awesome military power frustrated and frightened Higgs and his troops.

The military had moved two thousand troops within two miles of the compound, ready for an assault, if necessary, after two days of softening up. Since they were attacking fellow countrymen, they wanted to give them every opportunity to surrender.

When the shelling eventually stopped, Higgs had a few scouts venture out cautiously from the safe underground haven to try to determine if another assault was imminent.

At dawn, twenty helicopter gunships opened fire on the scouts. The first scout screamed, "I'm hit!"

Two other scouts were wounded, and five were killed. The gunships raked the entire camp with their guns blazing for a half hour. When they returned to the base, the shelling resumed.

Higgs and his followers were starting to see the futility of their situation. The South African military had them pinned down in their underground holes. Higgs could see the frustration and the fright in his followers' eyes and faces. There was not going to be an assault anytime soon. This was going to be an operation utilizing attrition and psychological warfare. They knew that troops would eventually move in, but they were in no hurry.

The rebels were not going to get any sleep, and they could not venture outside of their underground shelters. They were going to have to hole up like rodents until the troops were right on top of them. The only alternative to fighting was to surrender, which they had vowed not to do since Higgs and the hijackers would be tried, convicted, and sent to jail.

In the twenty-second hour of the attack, the troops were feeling even more vulnerable. They had no heavy guns or machine guns to ward off the attacks.

Higgs thought, *All our strategic planning did not prepare us for this kind of military strategy. We have to rethink our plans and determine how we are going to combat this assault. We're doomed.*

The big guns had been destroyed, and they could not survey the situation around them. The radio tower was gone, and they could not broadcast a plea for help from sympathizers. The bombardment continued, and the troops just sat in the underground shelters and bunkers.

Mortar fire and the occasional raking of the compound by helicopter gunships replaced the big guns of the military. The troops had moved up to within a mile of the compound. Commando squads had cut through the barbed wire so the advancing troops would not be deterred.

Higgs and his troops were totally pinned down. He realized that the South African military strategists could send troops in before dawn to capture the compound, but the strategists realized that an all-out assault would result in heavy casualties for both sides. They felt that such an assault would be counterproductive. The goal was to bring Higgs and the hijackers to justice, but it was equally as important to bring the different factions in the country together. High casualties on either side would not help the cause of uniting South Africa.

The strategists decided that the commandos would slip in and out of the camp to blow up the bunkers, supply stations, and other strategic structures. They would try to find the water supplies, food supplies, generators, ammunition supplies, and other support materials. The commandos moved in and out of the compound with practically no casualties on either side. They were accomplishing their missions, and the strategy was working.

Higgs moved his machine gunners to positions that he felt the commandos would be coming from. Higgs tried in vain to ward off the assault, but with high-powered telescopic surveillance, the commandos knew where the machine guns were aimed and avoided them for the most part.

As night fell, Higgs surveyed his beleaguered soldiers. He wiped the sweat from his forehead and approached a young soldier. "How long has this been going on?"

The soldier replied, "About sixty-six hours, sir. The siege has been ongoing for sixty-six hours now."

The soldiers steadied themselves in preparation for another onslaught.

Higgs surveyed the underground shelter and said, "We've been lucky so far, just a few men lost and wounded."

At nighttime, the bombardment continued. It was a nightmare for Higgs and his troops. There had not been many deaths or casualties, but the pounding was completely unnerving them.

Abruptly, the big guns stopped. Higgs and his troops knew something awful was about to happen. They began to prepare for a major assault. They looked out with their night-vision telescopes, but they didn't see or hear anything.

Fifty commandos inched silently across the compound. They were dressed in black camouflage uniforms, and their weapons were also painted black. The commandos who were not black wore black paint on their faces. All of the commandos wore black sweater caps. Each commando unit was in place, and all commandos were wearing gas masks. At the specified time, anesthetizing gas canisters were fired into the underground shelters.

Pandemonium broke out underground. Troops scrambled around in the dark, trying to locate their gas masks. They thought they were prepared, but the anesthetic gas spread so quickly and was so pervasive that it was too late for the majority of the troops.

Higgs got his mask on, but he was so lightheaded that he was unable to lift his Uzi when the commandos dropped down into the underground bunkers.

With just a few shots fired, the South African troops had captured the compound. The mission was over in less than three days.

Spotlights were brought up, and troops surrounded the compound. The rebels were brought to the surface, loaded into trucks, and taken away.

Higgs and the hijackers, once identified, were brought to the commanding general. They were arrested and taken into custody to be turned over to the South African police.

Higgs said, "The only regret I have is that we did not succeed. I wish I had more troops and support for the Freedom Alliance. I will never give up on getting a Volkstat."

CHAPTER 32

The Fantastic Six returned to Fort Bragg to receive a hero's welcome. There were citations, medals, and awards for them all. Praise came from every government and public arena. The president summoned them to the White House for a ceremony. Colonel Marvin Tate, Major Bonita Taylor, Captain Donna Rhodes, Sergeant Eddie Jackson, Corporal Harry Washington, and Corporal Tarik Booker were the toast of America. All the major TV networks carried their story, and Congress honored them. They were America's warrior heroes.

In South Africa, Renée, Michelle, Tina, and Denise sat by the embassy swimming pool and enjoyed a glass of Moscato Blanc with Renée's parents. The other parents had returned to their homes after being assured by Ambassador and Mrs. Davis that they would be perfectly safe and could resume their vacation plans. President Mandela had gone on television a few days earlier to announce the capture of the kidnappers and hijackers. The girls were talking about their harrowing experience and sharing the details they could remember. They told their story over and over again.

Now at ease, Horace sat calmly petting his dog as he listened to the girls. During a moment of tranquility, Horace's thoughts drifted. The girls' expressive accounts gently muffled into the back of his mind. *I don't know what I would have done if something had happened to Renée and the girls. South Africa is still so dangerous. The kidnapping just brought to light for me all the hell that South Africa has been through—and is still going through.* He looked up at his family. *We really have to be on our guard at all times out here. The people who are against the change to democracy are going to do everything possible to get some sort of power and some sort of control.* He drank his wine and stared off into the distance as the girls talked excitedly.

Beverly laughed at something the girls said, which jolted Horace from his thoughts. His attention returned to the conversation about the inauguration and the girls' plans for the rest of their vacation. For this moment, at least, the world was safe.

THE FANTASTIC SIX

Colonel Marvin Tate

Major Bonita Taylor

Sergeant Eddie Jackson

Corporal Harry Washington

Captain Donna Rhodes

Corporal Tariku Booker

About the Author

Harvey J. Williams, a well-respected Los Angeles orthodontist and gifted singer, competently takes on the literary world with his first creative work, the action-packed thriller *The Ambassador's Daughter*. There aren't too many life pleasures that give you an adrenaline rush like a great action-packed storyline where conflict between good and evil unravel and cause magnetic anticipation. In *The Ambassador's Daughter*, Williams presents an alluring challenge for readers of all ages to decipher the line he's drawn between truth and fiction. For more information, visit www.theambassadorsdaughter.com.

Printed in the United States
By Bookmasters